For eight years now *Perry Rhodan* has been acknowledged to be the world's top-selling science fiction series. Originally published in magazine form in Germany, the series has now appeared in hardback and paperback in the States.

Over five hundred *Perry Rhodan* clubs exist on the Continent and *Perry Rhodan* fan conventions are held annually. The first *Perry Rhodan* film, 'S.O.S. From Outer Space', has now also been released in Europe.

The series has sold over *140 million* copies in Europe alone.

Also available in the *Perry Rhodan* series

Walter Ernsting & Kurt Mahr

Perry Rhodan 4

Invasion from Space

Futura Publications Limited
An Orbit Book

An Orbit Book

First published in Great Britain in 1974
by Futura Publications Limited

Copyright © Ace Publishing Corporation 1970

The series was created by Walter Ernsting and
Karl-Herbert Scheer, and translated and edited
by Wendayne Ackerman.

ISBN 0 8600 7805 1
Printed in Great Britain by
Hazell Watson & Viney Ltd
Aylesbury, Bucks

Futura Publications Limited
49 Poland Street,
London W1A 2LG

INVASION FROM SPACE

CHAPTER ONE

Suddenly the man's eyes opened wide in utter horror, as if they had seen something beyond human comprehension. His eyes gazed up into the void, far into the depths of the blue sky that mirrored itself in the clear waters of the little pond in the woods. Then the expression of his eyes turned into a fixed and vacant stare.

There was not the slightest tremor in his hand, which was holding a fishing rod. His hand seemed to have become like stone. The man did not react when the swimmer was abruptly pulled deep below the surface of the water. The rod bent under the sudden strain for which Sammy Derring had been waiting so eagerly and in vain all morning long.

If anyone had looked into his eyes at this moment they would have recoiled in terror at the sight of such horrendous fright, mixed with inconceivable amazement. This lasted for exactly five seconds.

During these five seconds nobody could have recognized in this man, Sammy Derring, statistical clerk, who had worked for many years at the Ministry of Defense of the Western Bloc and for whom all his colleagues and superiors had nothing but praise. He was a bachelor, and his hobby was fishing. Every weekend he drove out to this little lake in the woods, where he caught some trout for his landlady. He did not care for fish, but he believed in the therapeutic effect of fishing. Very soothing for the nerves. His little sports car was parked off to the side—Sam's other hobby. He had only these two vices.

During the course of those five seconds, Sammy Derring could have been regarded as good as dead. His mind, his reasoning power, his soul, or whatever else people might call it, had left his body. Not of its own free will. It had been forced to do so. Something incomprehensible and far stronger had taken possession of his brain, had simply invaded it and pushed out what had been in there before.

During these five unbelievable seconds Sammy Derring could observe himself sitting at the lakeshore. He floated invisibly at a height of about fifteen feet and looked down on himself. He was unable to comprehend what was happening, but he simply saw his own body, as if he had become a stranger to his own self. He saw that he appeared to be dead but that he remained sitting there. Shouldn't he have toppled over? His body should by all rights have fallen down on the ground. But no. There he was, still sitting upright at the edge of the water, unaware that the fish were biting!

Sammy's mind felt an urge to pull in the fishing rod, but the body down below no longer obeyed his thought impulses. But there was no more time left for all this. The five seconds were over. The picture of the peaceful little lake in the woods became hazy and soon disappeared completely for him as an invisible force yanked him away. He became dimly aware of a wild kaleidoscope of colors. For an instant he thought he saw, way down below, a huge globe, but then everything turned dark. He felt drawn into something; then all of a sudden his reflexes returned. He could feel his body and his limbs, and he was able to move them.

Now he could see again despite the darkness around him. Then he noticed that it was not totally dark. The room was filled with a faint glow. He wondered for a moment how on Earth he had come to this place. But then it did not really matter to him any more. He must have had some seizure, and they had taken him to the hospital. That must be it! He was ill. A great weakness overwhelmed him. Wasn't there anyone here to take care of him? He sensed that somebody was nearby. With great effort he tried to sit up, but he could not manage it. Had this sudden sickness overcome him while he was fishing at the little lake? Had people found him there and brought him here? How long had he been unconscious?

And how had all this really happened? Hadn't he seen

himself sitting down there at the lakeshore? Now his eyes had become adjusted to the dark and he could see again. But his weakness grew worse. He felt himself going to sleep. But there was something still active and wide awake in his brain, something that would not let him fall asleep—some observation he had made. It took a long time, precious seconds, before it reached his center of awareness and then changed into stark, maddening reality.

His fingers . . . his legs!

With his remaining strength he opened his eyes wide for a last look and gazed, full of horror, at the ends of his four arms, at the sharp claws with suction pads. . . .

And then he perceived the trunk of his body, like that of a wasp with a very narrow waist, all covered with fine hair. The gruesome shape of the monster to which he had been transformed so swiftly impressed him as being so unreal that he closed his black multifaceted insect eyes with a sigh of relief and stretched out his legs.

Of course! It was only a nightmare! Why hadn't he thought of that sooner!

But the sudden flash of insight, that man never knows he is only dreaming while he is having a nightmare, came too late.

His mind, held captive in an extraterrestrial body, sank into a deathlike trance. . . .

As soon as the five seconds had elapsed Sammy Derring reeled in the line of his fishing rod. He stared at the fat trout without any special interest; then, after some initial hesitation, he pulled it off the hook and threw it back into the water. He flung the rod carelessly into the bushes growing near the edge of the water and began to walk toward the car parked nearby. His gait was unsteady as if he had been sick in bed for weeks. When he reached his car he hesitated again for a brief moment, just as long as it took to obtain all the necessary information from the memory banks of the intellect that had inhabited this body before him.

Sammy Derring, who in reality was no longer Sammy Derring, started the car and drove slowly along the bumpy side road until he reached the main highway. There a swift

7

glance at the road signs was sufficient. A few minutes later the little sports car raced toward the city.

Mrs. Sarah Wabble was not a little surprised to see her tenant return so early from his weekly fishing expedition. But her amazement grew when he simply nodded to her and then went straight to his rooms, where he locked the door behind him. No friendly greeting and no trout, either!

The being that was now Sammy Derring felt much relieved as soon as the door had closed behind him. Now he was safe from these human creatures. His experience in taking over the bodies of other organisms was still rather limited. In addition to that, the inhabitants of this planet were of a rather high intelligence, intelligence difficult to remove and to conserve. It would have been so much simpler to eliminate them entirely, but that would have been contrary to his commander's strict orders.

His commander had not come down to this planet's surface. He was far out in space in an oval shaped spaceship that was revolving around the third planet of this solar system, invisible to these humans' eyes. This glittering metallic spacecraft had not been designed and built by human hands, but by extraterrestrial, nonhuman insect claws provided with suction pads, which were no less skillful than five-fingered human extremities. The intelligence that guided the movements of the six jointed limbs of the almost seven foot long insects, which somehow resembled wasps, was at about the same level as that of the Earthlings. But considering certain mental abilities of these insectlike creatures, it was safe to say that the wasps were far superior to the human race.

One of their talents was the amazing ability that enabled the minds of these extraterrestrial beings to leave their own bodies and take over those of other creatures. It was like a regular exchange. They simply snatched the other beings' minds and replaced them with their own.

But all knowing Nature had made sure that there remained one weak spot in this forced mind exchange. The mind of the seized host body could be subdued and captured only if it was imprisoned for the duration in the insect's own body. Only then full freedom of action was ensured for the mindsnatcher, who could do anything he wanted in his new body, pretending to be the victim himself. In case the host died before it was possible to leave his body, the mindsnatcher died too. And it was also fatal if the insect body that held the victim's mind imprisoned was destroyed. Both host and victim lost their life in either case.

Despite the limitations, these sinister insects were one of the most dangerous races of the universe. But the Earthlings had no inkling of that peril; not too long ago they had made their first step out into space by landing a rocket on the moon. Earth was like a lonely island in the sea of space, isolated from the happenings in the universe, believing itself all alone. Mankind knew nothing of the many intelligent races of the galaxies, of the galactic empires that had been founded and then destroyed again.

But the extraterrestrial races who knew these insects and their uncanny abilities called them the Mindsnatchers, or the M.S., for short.

And now the M.S. had located Earth. This so far completely unknown planet at the edge of the Milky Way had suddenly become the center of events of a magnitude that could not yet be fully evaluated. The M.S. had been attracted by the emergency signals of an Arkonide cruiser. The Arkonides, masters of a vast realm of the stars, were the archenemies of the wasp creatures. It was impossible to conquer them in battle, unless the insects could track their ships down individually and then attack them.

Such a rare opportunity seemed to have presented itself in this case. One of the Arkonide research vessels must have made an emergency landing in this solar system. But to the great surprise of the M.S., it had turned out that the third planet from this sun was inhabited by a rather intelligent race, which had developed a technology capable of space travel. Therefore, it was high time to investigate them, before the Arkonides would do so.

This was the reason why the M.S. commander had ordered Terra to be infiltrated. He was absolutely sure that he could seize the most important organizations and key positions of Earth's political, economic, and scientific institutions within a short time.

He had given the orders for the invasion.

But mankind was unaware of all of this. All they knew was that some strange spaceship had appeared and had been destroyed. But they did not realize that the M.S. had come to their part of the solar system with more than just one spaceship. And in particular they had no idea, except for a few select people, who these M.S. were and what they intended.

Monday morning Sammy Derring came to work as usual at the Ministry of Defense. No one could have detected any change in him as far as his looks were concerned. He entered his office and was soon busy rummaging through file cabinets examining all kinds of papers. Then suddenly he sounded a buzzer to call in his secretary.

The young girl entered, ready to take the usual dictation. But Sammy simply shook his head and requested in all earnestness, "Will you bring me all records and documents pertaining to the national defense system. Then also all data regarding our present status of space exploration and rocket development. I am particularly interested in the effectiveness of our defense plans. . . . Don't stare at me like that! Get a move on!"

The secretary swallowed hard and blushed. "Pardon me, Mr. Derring—"

"Didn't you hear me the first time? Hurry up!"

She was about to reply, when she noticed the look in Sammy's eyes. Their expression was so faraway and strange that she shuddered involuntarily. Totally consternated she just nodded and went out of the room, leaving behind a very contented Sammy Derring, or rather something that looked like him.

Outside the door in her office, the secretary stopped for a moment as if rooted to the spot. Then she vigorously shook her head and walked straight over to her department manager, John Mantell.

Mantell listened attentively to what the young secretary had to tell him. Finally he frowned, and replied, "Are you sure that Mr. Derring wasn't kidding?"

"I am absolutely sure. He was dead serious. And then . . . this strange expression in his eyes. I have never seen such a frightening look. Never, in all my life."

Mantell contemplated his immaculately manicured fingernails. "Odd, very odd indeed. He wants to examine all the records of our national defense system. He certainly must know that such documents are accessible only to the

Secretary of Defense, but never to an ordinary statistical clerk."

He looked up and smiled ironically at the pretty young girl. "Do you think that Mr. Derring might have lost his mind? He seems to be getting too big for his britches."

For the first time the secretary dared smile back at her supervisor. "For all we know, he might believe that there is more than just a mere resemblance in their names! He told me once in a joking way that he and the Secretary of Defense had similar names, that someday they might even be mistaken for each other. . . ."

"I don't believe that Samuel Daring would take too kindly to such remarks," commented Mantell. "I'll have to set Sammy straight on this. Tell him to come to see me at eleven o'clock, will you?"

She hesitated. "But what shall I tell him now about the files he wants me to bring him?"

"Oh, whatever you want. I'm busy. Don't bother me any more."

Slowly the secretary left the room, but she did not return to her own office. For a few minutes she stood out in the hall, trying to make up her mind what to do. Then suddenly she turned on her heel and marched directly into the lion's den, to the special agent attached to her bureau in the Ministry of Defense.

Mr. Smith was quite astonished when he heard her story. He considered the matter far more serious than Mr. Mantell had. Mantell had most likely already forgotten the whole incident by now, but the Commissioner of Defense requested the secretary to come to his office and wait at his receptionist's desk for a while. As soon as she was out of his private office, he became very busy. He took a telephone from a wall safe, dialed a number, and then waited impatiently. Finally he reached his party.

"This is Smith speaking from the Ministry of Defense. Something very strange has happened, sir. Most irregular, unless somebody was just trying to be funny. But I received your instructions three days ago that I should investigate and inform you of any unusual behavior—"

He was interrupted by the person he was conversing with. A precise question was addressed to him. Smith trembled slightly and sat up stiffly in his chair. He appeared to have great respect for the man at the other end of the line.

"Very well, sir. One of our statistical clerks, Sammy Derring, requested our secret national defense plans. Besides, he demanded all information regarding the state of our space exploration program. He made these demands in all seriousness. His secretary told me that she has never before noticed such determination in him. And she was especially disturbed by the odd expression in Sammy Derring's eyes."

Again there came an interruption. But this time so loud that it could be heard even without the receiver, if anyone had been standing next to Smith.

"What is his name, did you say?"

"Sammy Derring, sir."

"And what is the name of the Secretary of Defense?"

"Uh, Samuel Daring, sir. But you certainly know that yourself, sir."

"Thanks, Smith. Here are my instructions: Act as if nothing unusual had happened. Tell the secretary to bring Derring the requested papers, but of course, only those that are out of date. Derring must not become suspicious. Do you get this?"

"Yes, sir. Anything else?"

"Don't breathe a word to anyone about all this! I'll be over at your office within two hours."

"You are going to come here in person?" Smith was overawed. That was unheard of! Allan D. Mercant, the mighty chief of the Western Defense and of the International Intelligence Agency, would fly over and investigate this affair! Such a piddling little incident! Probably it would all turn out to be just a silly joke that Sammy Derring had thought up in order to impress his secretary because his name resembled that of the Secretary of Defense.

"Yes. I'll fly over to investigate what's behind all this. And better make sure not to let anyone know of it! That goes for the little secretary too! Absolute secrecy! That will be all for now."

Smith replaced the phone in the wall safe. A pensive frown lay around his eyes as he called for the secretary. As she entered the room he motioned to a chair and then said in a matter of fact tone of voice, "Don't talk to anyone about what happened with Mr. Derring. He is probably

12

. . . well, let's say . . . sick. Maybe some kind of delusion of grandeur. In about ten minutes I'll have a stack of files sent to your office. Please give those to Mr. Derring. Is that clear?"

"Yes, but—"

"Don't worry! You just tell Mr. Derring that the papers are on their way to him. And may I remind you once again—don't let anyone know what has happened."

The little secretary could not help but remember having already told someone about Sammy Derring's strange request. She had spoken to her department manager, Mantell, before she came to the Commissioner. But Mantell obviously hadn't been interested in her complaint. Maybe he had even forgotten all by now. So she simply nodded.

"Yes, Mr. Smith. I understand. I'll give the message to Mr. Derring. I only hope he won't look so odd and frightening again. He half scared me to death."

"Oh, nonsense, Miss . . . ?"

"Thompson. Clara Thompson."

"There is no need to be afraid, Miss Thompson. Mr. Derring seems to be suffering from a temporary delusion. It was pretty hot yesterday, and he might have got too much sun. Maybe a slight sun stroke."

Clara Thompson did not quite agree with the Commissioner of Defense. She could not accept such a lame excuse for someone suddenly believing he was the Secretary of Defense. But she did not speak up. After all, who was she to tell the big boss what was right or wrong? So she left and returned to her own office. She forgot all about Mr. Mantell.

Sammy looked up when she entered. "Well, are you bringing the documents I requested?"

"They will be sent over in ten minutes."

"Thanks. Bring them right in, as soon as they arrive."

"I will, Mr. Derring."

Clara could not get the door closed behind her soon enough. She felt ill at ease in his presence. Still, he appeared quite sensible, no more scary look in his eyes. Yet he still insisted on this idiotic order for the secret documents.

Ten minutes later a messenger brought the files. They were in a big red envelope marked, TOP SECRET.

Miss Thompson stared at the envelope. How important it looked! So impressive with the TOP SECRET stamp. But she knew that in reality its contents were completely worthless. Why was the Commissioner of Defense going along with that stupid request? It seemed childish to humor an employee who had lost his marbles. Or could there be more to the whole affair than met the eye?

She took the envelope, knocked at Mr. Derring's door, and entered. Without a word she placed the big red envelope on his desk and looked at him, waiting for an acknowledgment. She noticed a gleam of triumph in his eyes. But there was something additional again, something that she could not interpret—something faraway and bottomless. It was as if she were gazing into an abyss so deep that one could fall through it forever, into eternity. Confused, she turned away and left the room abruptly.

Sammy Derring waited until the door had closed behind her; then he opened the envelope and began examining its contents. A first glance told him that his mission had been successful. There they were, right in front of him, the greatest secrets of this world . . . or at least those of one of the big power blocs. In other parts of this planet other M.S. would be just as effective in their efforts. By tomorrow the commander would be informed about the defense potential of this planet's population and the best strategy for starting an invasion. For it was not enough simply to take over the bodies of these clumsy two-legged creatures. They had to be made subservient to the rule of their new masters. To all outward appearances, though, they had to remain independent.

While he was perusing the documents he noted with satisfaction that he had greatly overestimated the potential of the Terrans.

It was almost eleven o'clock. A few doors down the hall John Mantell suddenly remembered the conversation he had had with Sammy Derring's secretary. For a moment he hesitated. Perhaps he should forget about the whole thing and not waste his precious time with the foolish jokes of one of his subalterns. But then his sense of duty won out. After all, such silly pranks occasionally turned into serious problems. Better stop that nonsense at once, before it went too far. He pressed the buzzer of the intercom. A young girl's voice replied.

"Miss Thompson? What's the matter with Derring? Didn't you tell him that I want to see him here in my office at eleven o'clock?"

Clara had almost forgotten about Mr. Mantell. She stammered, "Oh, no, Mr. Mantell, I haven't forgotten. But maybe it would be better to ignore this incident? I am sure Mr. Derring was just making a harmless joke. I don't want him to get into any trouble. . . ."

"Then you shouldn't have come to me in the first place. Well then, are you going to give him my message or not?"

"I . . . I . . ."

Puzzled, Mantell flipped a switch on the intercom to terminate that disquieting conversation. He got up with determination and left his office to walk over to Derring's room. Ten seconds later he encountered Clara Thompson as she was just about to leave her own office. She was startled and scared when she saw Mantell.

"What's wrong? Where are you going?"

Her confusion seemed to grow worse. She could hardly bring out the words, "To . . . to . . . to see you, Mr. Mantell. I was coming over to ask you if that visit could wait. Mr. Derring is awfully busy right now. I can't disturb him when he has important work to do."

Mantell's eyebrows shot up. "Important work? You don't say! This I have got to see for myself!"

He shoved Miss Thompson aside, and without even bothering to knock he stormed into Derring's room. There he saw his subaltern, busily poring over a stack of papers. Annoyed at the sudden interruption he glowered at the intruder, obviously not understanding what all this was supposed to mean. It was five seconds before a glimmer of comprehension lit up his face.

"Oh, yes, Mr. Mantell. What can I do for you?"

Mantell banged a fist on Sammy's desk. "Are you out of your mind, Derring? What can *you* do for *me*? How dare you pull such stupid tricks on our personnel, asking this poor little girl to bring you our most secret documents! You act as if you think you are the Secretary of Defense in person! And even he himself is not authorized to . . .

What is the matter with you, Derring? Are you feeling all right?"

An alarming change had overcome Sammy Derring. First his eyes gazed uncomprehendingly at the raging department manager; then his eyes became empty and lost their luster. When his eyes seemed to see again, they were filled with a steely lack of pity. He asked with an icy cold voice, "What is the name of the Secretary of Defense?"

Mantell gasped. This was more than he could take. "Derring! Have you gone crazy? Now you want me to believe you don't remember the name of our Secretary of Defense?"

Sammy nodded, apparently unperturbed by the enormity of his *faux pas.* "Yes. I don't know his name. What is it?"

Although Mantell was unwilling to comply with every wish of the obviously insane clerk, the steely eyes of the man behind the desk seemed to compel him to do so nevertheless. He shouted, "Daring, Samuel Daring. You of all people should know this better than I. This isn't the first time that you have run into trouble because your names were mistaken for each other, Sammy Derring! But this is no excuse whatsoever . . ."

Mantell fell silent before he could finish his tirade, for Sammy Derring jumped to his feet, pointing to the documents lying in front of him on his desk.

"And if I am not the Secretary of Defense, why did they send me the records I requested?"

Mantell looked at the papers, the envelope marked TOP SECRET in particular. He could not understand this. But before he had a chance to say anything, the door flew open. In came Smith, Clara Thompson close behind him. He quickly grasped the situation. There was an air of annoyance spread all over his face.

Mantell felt frightened. He knew that this inconspicuous looking man had been empowered with the final say in all matters concerning this section of the Ministry of Defense.

"What's all this supposed to mean? What is going on here?" inquired Smith, who could have given the answer perfectly well himself. He addressed Mantell. "Didn't Miss Thompson pass on my orders to you not to interfere in this affair?"

"He wouldn't listen to me," explained Clara Thompson.

"She came and told me that Mr. Derring was trying to play a silly joke," defended Mantell. "I only wanted to ask Derring to stop such tomfoolery in the future. The resemblance of his name to that of the Secretary of Defense does not entitle him to—"

No one had been paying any attention to what Sammy Derring was doing in the meantime. He sat down again, and all life seemed to fade from his eyes. He was sitting behind his desk, head held high. His eyes gazed just as expressionlessly into space as they had done the day before, staring up into the empty blue sky above the little lake in the woods. This lasted exactly five seconds. Then it was over. Life returned to his eyes.

During these five seconds the same process had taken place as twenty-four hours earlier, but in reverse. The M.S. had fled from his host's body, after having recognized he had fallen victim to a case of mistaken identity. He acted rather panic stricken, for he could have smoothed over his mistake if he had tried to. But he preferred to return to his sleeping body and to release from it the imprisoned mind of Sammy Derring. Sammy's intellect returned to his own body. He lacked any memory of what had befallen him except for a few insignificant details that seemed more like a dream.

Hadn't he just been sitting at the lake, holding his fishing rod? How was it possible that he was now sitting behind his desk in his office? He saw his department manager, Mantell, standing before him, next to him the Commissioner of Defense in person . . . and over there at the door pretty little Clara Thompson contemplating him with consternation in her big blue eyes.

Why could he not remember the last twenty-four hours? What had happened during this time?

"Can I help you, gentlemen?" he inquired mechanically. Then he noticed the open files on his desk. He was puzzled by the red envelope marked TOP SECRET. Without understanding he stared from the files to his visitors.

"What are these files doing here? How did they get here?"

Before Mantell could give expression to the fury raging in him, Smith intervened. His clear mind was capable of lightning fast reactions. Although he did not understand the reasons behind this incident, he recalled that his superior, Allan D. Mercant, was on his way to this office. And there must be compelling reasons for him to inconvenience himself by flying over here all the way from his base in Greenland. There must be more to this harmless appearing affair than met the eye.

"These are some old reports, long since out of date, Mr. Derring. Would you please check them over. The Secretary of Defense requested that some reliable employee be charged with this confidential task."

Sammy still appeared perplexed, but he answered eagerly, "Thank you for the confidence you have in me. I certainly won't disappoint you. How long will I have for this job?"

"There is no special hurry, Mr. Derring. Come now, Mr. Mantell. And you, too, Miss Thompson. Let Mr. Derring get on with his work now!"

He pulled the utterly startled Mantell by the arm and walked him to the door, which he held open for the little secretary scurrying after the two men.

As soon as the door had closed behind the trio Smith breathed a deep sigh of relief. "It seems to have turned out all right after all. Listen, Mantell! You almost messed up the whole affair. I really couldn't tell you what's behind this, but Mr. Mercant is on his way here."

"The Chief of Western Defense? The big boss of the International Intelligence Agency? Did I understand you correctly, Mr. Smith? But that can't be!" The words came in rapid fire succession out of the amazed Mantell.

"That's the way it is, Mantell," said Smith. "Go back to your office and don't bother any more about Derring. That's an order! The Secretary of Defense will not learn about this regrettable incident, so don't worry. And the same goes for you, Miss Thompson. Just keep quiet about this. I'll explain everything to you tonight over a nice dinner."

"But I—"

"Would eight o'clock be all right? I'll call at your house—just leave the address with my secretary. O.K.?"

"I—"

"Fine! And now sit down at your desk and act as if nothing had happened. And if you look at it, nothing really did happen, did it?"

While the stratoliner from Greenland was flying at Mach

three toward his destination, the Ministry of Defense of the Western Bloc, and while Mercant was evaluating and speculating about the suspicious incident with Sammy Derring, the latter was sitting at his desk, checking the long since outdated documents, puzzled by this senseless task, wondering why he of all persons had been charged with it.

As far as he could recall he had just been spending the weekend fishing for trout at his favorite spot at the little lake in the nearby forest. How on Earth he had suddenly been transported from there to his desk in the office was a mystery to him. True, there had been some strange moments, he remembered now. Kind of a daydream. And then the big, dark cave with . . . with . . . oh, yes—that's right! With some monster that looked like a giant wasp. And he himself had been that wasp. Ridiculous! Had he lost his mind? But then he wouldn't be sitting here now in his office, being entrusted with some special, highly confidential task by his superiors.

He sighed and decided to stop thinking about this whole silly thing. If he began asking all kinds of questions that would merely arouse unnecessary suspicions. And the office here would not have any use for him, if he brought up such crazy stuff. Nightmares or daydreams, whatever it was, he must have been asleep, for he could absolutely not remember anyone bringing these secret documents to him.

Blond hair ringed the bald dome of the incredibly young appearing man whose harmless face reminded an observer of some peaceful nature lover. His innocuous appearance was quite deceptive, though, for he was one of the most feared and respected men of the Western Bloc. Until a few short weeks ago all the agents of the Eastern Bloc and those of the Asiatic Federation had trembled at the mere mention of his name.

Allan D. Mercant, chief of the NATO Defense, was preparing himself for an encounter with a man whose body had been taken over by an M.S. This was not the first time he had met one of the M.S. Only a few days had passed since an M.S. had tried to put him out of action in the disguise of one of Mercant's closest collaborators whose body he had assumed. Only thanks to Mercant's rapid re-actions and his faint telepathy had he escaped unscathed.

The invasion, expected by only a handful of persons, seemed to have begun. Although it had been expected, the invasion still came as a surprise. This apparent contra-diction could be explained. An alien spaceship belonging to the M.S. had been destroyed near the moon's orbital path, and most people assumed that this was the only space-craft the invaders had inside this solar system. Mankind prepared itself for further attacks but did not really believe they would occur.

Without the help of the Third Power, mankind would perish. Mercant was fully aware of this. The first manned expedition to the moon under the command of Perry Rhodan had found there the crash-landed interstellar research craft of a highly intelligent but decadent alien race. The sci-entific leader of this research project, a certain Khrest, had become dangerously ill with leukemia. He had been cured by the Earthlings, especially with the help of Dr. Haggard, the world's greatest specialist in blood diseases. The Arkonides, as the aliens called themselves, originated from a system thirty-two thousand light-years from Sol. They were searching for the legendary planet of eternal life. The only two surviving members of the Arkonide expedition, Khrest and Thora, became allies of Rhodan. Together they founded the Third Power, whose base was in the Gobi Desert. This Third Power had managed, within three short months, to unite the three formerly hostile power blocs of the world. Then the first attack from outer space oc-curred. The M.S. had intercepted the emergency signals broadcast by the destroyed Arkonide spaceship on the moon. The M.S. had come hurriedly in order to administer the final blow to their age-old enemies, the Arkonides. But the M.S. had encountered unexpected resistance from the so far unknown Earthlings and had suffered a crushing de-feat at their hands.

This was the way things stood now. Perry Rhodan was the only person capable of saving the world. Mercant knew this only too well. Although the three power blocs did not yet fully trust Rhodan, they were on the other hand afraid of the M.S. and of the Arkonide weapons that were at Rhodan's disposal. Then there was something else that only

a few initiated knew, besides Mercant—Rhodan had succeeded in gathering in several mutants that had been born
as a result of the post-World War II atom bomb explosions.
These mutants, whose abilities needed further schooling,
formed the nucelus of a new troop that Rhodan had organ-
ized for the protection of the Third Power. Because of his
telepathic talents, Mercant belonged to this mutant corps.
But this was known only to the two men, Rhodan and
Mercant himself, besides the other members of the secret
mutant organization.

The plane landed. A fast moving car brought Mercant
to the Ministry of Defense. He was led to Smith, who
was waiting for him in his private office.

"Well, Smith, what has happened? Where is he?"

"He doesn't have the faintest idea, sir. Shall I take you
to him?"

"Yes, please."

Smith was very surprised to see Mercant take a gun out
of his shoulder holster, release the safety catch, and then
put it calmly into his pocket. He intended to tell Mercant
that there had never lived a more harmless person than
Sammy Derring, but then he thought better of it and kept
silent. He led the way without a word. Mercant followed
behind, not speaking either.

Sammy Derring looked up, startled when the door was
suddenly pushed open. He recognized Smith, but he was
sure he had never met the harmless looking man before. But
as he noted a little while later, the man was not as harmless
as he had appeared at first sight. His eyes seemed to be
lying in ambush for something.

"Sammy Derring?" the unknown asked softly. "Just stay
seated and don't move. Answer my questions without hesitation. At the slightest suspicious move on your part I'll
shoot you. My name is Mercant."

Sammy was nonplussed. His face assumed an indescrib-
ably stupid grimace. His mouth gaped, and he stared clumsily into the dark barrel of the gun that Mercant was pointing at him.

"What do you want from me?" he managed to squeeze
out.

"Why did you request the secret files to which only
the Defense Minister has access?"

"Secret files? I did not request them. They were brought to me by Mr. Smith and Mr. Mantell. I am supposed to check them over. I wouldn't dream of requesting such secret documents. It is totally out of the question that I would do such a thing."

"So you say they were brought to you? And you definitely deny having requested them?"

"I know nothing at all about this whole affair. Anyhow, everything seems to me like in a dream. Everything is so strange."

"Will you explain this a bit more in detail, Mr. Derring," urged Mercant, leaning forward with an expression of intense concentration. Smith stood next to him.

Sammy hesitated. The whole story seemed so odd to him, and now he was supposed to tell it to his superiors. How would they accept such a fantastic tale?

"I was fishing," he began. And noticing the amazed look on Mercant's face he added swiftly, "I was fishing yesterday at my favorite spot at a little lake in the woods. Suddenly a strange sensation came over me. I felt as if I could leave my own body, and that's exactly what I did. A few seconds later I was in a big, dark cave. For a moment I thought I had seen Earth lying deep down below me. It was a crazy dream. Then I woke up, and I was sitting here in my office and Mr. Smith had just brought these documents to me. That is the truth, the whole truth, even if I can't explain it to myself. I don't know what went on in the interval."

"That happens once in a while," Mercant admitted politely. "But in your case it would be advisable to find out what you have done in the past twenty-four hours that seem to have slipped from your memory."

"Maybe my landlady could help you there. We could ask her."

"That's a good idea. We will follow that up." Mercant gave some instructions. Smith went out to the secretary's little office. Five minutes later he came back.

"Mr. Derring was home last night. He returned earlier than usual from his fishing trip, without bringing any fish to his landlady. That's the first time that ever happened, according to Mrs. Wabble, his landlady. Mr. Derring seemed not his usual self, very odd, and went straight to bed.

This morning she could not detect anything out of the ordinary in her lodger's behavior."

Mercant looked at Derring. "Can you swear to it that you are again your own self?"

"Can I swear to *what?*"

"I want to know if you feel normal again. It is obvious that there is a gap in your memory. From yesterday afternoon until about two hours ago you were doing and saying things which you can't recall now. Something else had taken over your body and pretended to be you."

"But that is—"

"Yes, it is possible, contrary to what you may believe. Not for any human being, of course, but you might have heard that there are other living beings in the universe besides ourselves."

"Yes, I have heard about the Arkonides."

"No, not the Arkonides. I am talking about the M.S., an insectlike race that know how to snatch a person's mind from his body and replace it with their own minds. In your particular case, a case of mistaken identity has occurred. The M.S. who invaded your brain mistook you for the Secretary of Defense. Your names are almost alike. We don't yet know the M.S. methods of communicating with each other. It seems to be based on acoustics. Phonetic sounds, rather than writing. Daring sounds almost like Derring, particularly to some untrained alien ear, not familiar with the fine points of English pronunciation. The alien creature slipped into the wrong man. That's all. Mr. Derring, you have done a tremendous service to mankind, even if unintentionally, because of your name."

Mercant had put the gun back into his pocket long since. There was no longer any doubt in his mind that the M.S. must have left his host's body some time ago. But to his surprise, Sammy Derring seemed to be none the worse for his experience. He looked healthy and absolutely normal. Therefore, the theory must be wrong that nobody could survive such a mind snatching episode. But at the same time Mercant realized that the Secretary of Defense would be the next target for the M.S. He must be put under strict surveillance immediately. And Perry Rhodan had to be informed of these events immediately, before any further attacks could take place.

Mercant gave some more instructions to Smith. The agent disappeared to carry them out. He did not fully understand the game that was being played here, but he was used to carrying out orders promptly, regardless. He went straight to Miller, Daring's private secretary.

He found Miller in a turmoil of activity. Orders sounded over the intercom, messengers brought sealed envelopes, locked files were dragged up from the safes in the basement, and Miller waved impatiently when Smith dared speak to him. "Don't bother me now; come back at some other time. The boss has no time."

"Don't you know who I am?"

"Of course I do, but that doesn't matter any longer. Or have you come to arrest Mr. Daring?"

"Who knows," grinned Smith, seeing Miller gasp for air. "Just calm down for a moment. I have a few questions I would like to ask you."

"Be quick about it!"

"What's all the excitement about? What's all this dragging by of files and documents supposed to mean?"

"The Chief's personal orders. He requested all documents regarding national defense and rocket development. After all, he can't possibly carry *all* the data around in his head."

"Is that so?" asked Smith, and had disappeared before Miller could figure out what had taken place.

In the meantime Mercant had obtained a direct line to his headquarters in Greenland. From there a connection was established to Perry Rhodan's base in the Gobi Desert. Under the protective umbrella of an invisible shield lay the center of the Third Power, the latest power bloc on Earth, which had come into existence several months previously.

But to his great regret Mercant was told that Perry Rhodan was unavailable. He was on Venus, Earth's sister planet.

As Smith entered, Mercant was just ending his conversation. He looked up and said heavily, "Whatever is going to happen, Smith, we will have to carry the responsibility on our own shoulders. And now you can tell me that Samuel Daring, or whatever the thing is hiding in Samuel

Daring's body, has ordered all top secret files to be brought to him. Isn't that what you just found out?"

Thunderstruck, Smith managed only to nod.

CHAPTER TWO

The huge boulder lay on the flat surface of the desert plain. The sun was shining fiercely down on the rock. The air rose like a glimmering hot column, but nothing disturbed its shape, for there was not the slightest breeze to stir the burning air.

All of a sudden the incredible happened. The rock lifted off the ground as if a giant, invisible hand had picked it up. Infinitely slow, the boulder began to float. Now it was resting on some invisible ledge a foot above the desert floor; it kept rising.

If anyone had been able to watch this performance, he would have doubted his own sanity. The boulder weighed at least ten tons, but it behaved as if the laws of gravity had no application to it. It climbed upward like a gas-filled balloon, then moved a little distance sideways. Then it crashed down on the ground as if the invisible hand had suddenly released its grip. Dust rose whirling, then settled slowly again.

The boulder lay on the ground as if it had never moved in such a weird fashion. Once again the sun's rays hit it straight on, heating spots that shortly before had been covered by the cooling shade.

But this rest period did not last. The rock moved again, this time faster and more steadily. It rose up thirty feet into the air and then flew off sideways. Relentlessly it kept flying parallel to the flat surface of the desert floor, coming closer to the shore of a still salt lake whose waters lay quiet like a smooth mirror. Suddenly the boulder fell straight down into the lake, disappearing in a deep walled water funnel, leaving behind a series of concentric spreading waves that slowly ebbed away on reaching the shore.

Several people stood at a distance of more than a mile from the salt lake, gazing over to its blue expanse. The oldest of the group, a white haired giant with an unusually high domed skull and a pale complexion, nodded with satisfied mien. Next to him stood a young woman who made a gesture to signify her appreciation.

The short Japanese for whom this praise was intended merely shrugged his shoulders with embarrassment. "I bungled this job," he admitted without realizing how grossly he undervalued his capacities. "I simply can't do it, Miss Sloane."

The young girl, Anne Sloane, turned to the white haired man. "Never mind what Tama thinks about himself, Mr. Khrest. Tama is just too modest. According to the frequency detector he is a mutant, and I have no doubt that he is one indeed. He managed to raise a ten ton boulder at a distance of more than a mile for almost seven feet, using only the strength of his mind. He has telekinetic powers, even if they are only in the initial stage. I needed several years to perfect my abilities. Tama, you'll have to be a patient pupil to become as good as myself at this. Don't lose heart!"

The Arkonide scientist, who had crash landed on the moon and who had become Rhodan's collaborator, supervising all technical matters, tried to encourage Tama Yokida.

"Don't give up, Tama. You need more training, that's all. After all, you possess an additional talent that will permit you to develop into an extraordinary human being. Although Miss Sloane is a master at telekinesis, you can change an element into another and gather up the released energy at will and use it whichever way you want. That is a tremendously valuable ability. Together with your telekinetic predisposition, this will grow into a combination with a fantastic potential."

Tama Yokida continued smiling humbly as before. "You are right, Mr. Khrest. I should be grateful to nature for having endowed me with such unusual talents. Do you wish to continue the instruction now?"

Khrest gazed pensively out over the now calm surface of the salt lake. He placed a reassuring hand on the shoulder of the tiny Japanese. Then he spoke to Anne Sloane. "You let the rock fall down into the water, Miss Sloane. I am amazed at your telekinetic powers. I wonder if Tama will be able to influence the sunken boulder by way of telekinesis."

Anne glanced at the young Japanese before she replied. "I couldn't tell. As far as I am concerned I am positive that I could lift that rock out of the water again any time. Whether Tama can do this from this distance . . . The salt lake isn't too deep."

"How deep?" inquired Tama. "I would have to know."

Khrest spoke into a tiny all purpose apparatus that he wore as a wide band around his wrist. "Dr. Haggard? Would you be so kind and send Miss Ishi Matsu out to us here? That's right. For a lesson."

Anne Sloane understood. "Isn't that the little Japanese girl with the unusual gift of being able to see through solid bodies?"

"That's right," confirmed Khrest. "She is what I would call a televisionary. She can perceive the rock lying at the bottom of this lake and thus determine its depth. She, too, will have to receive further training in order to fully develop her talents. Once she is able to penetrate optically big parts of the earth's crust, our mutant corps will be able to function like a living television installation."

Tama smiled gently. "My little colleague and I complement each other splendidly," he confessed. "I hope the time will soon come when all of the mutants will learn to coordinate their efforts. Then no power on Earth will be able to resist us."

"I think we have already reached that point," countered Khrest, while directing his glance toward the conglomeration of low lying buildings that had sprung up around the hull of the first moon rocket, the *Stardust I*, which had landed here after its return from man's first successful moon expedition. An invisible energy dome covered the complex and the surrounding area of almost thirty square miles. The invisible barrier received its energy from the inexhaustible Arkonide reactions.

"We are not that deeply concerned with the mutant corps's ability to make a stand against other powers of this world," Khrest said, "but rather their ability to ward off attackers from space. The unfortunate emergency signals from our cruiser on this planet's moon will attract still more space traveling races. I am afraid Earth's isolated position in the universe has come to an end finally. Oh, here comes Miss Ishi."

27

A slender, delicate young girl came walking toward the group. She was wearing blue jeans and a white blouse that made her slim but perfectly shaped figure look most attractive. Tama Yokida was obviously very impressed by his lovely compatriot. It was clear to all present that the two young people felt something more than just casual friendship for each other.

"You have asked for me, Mr. Khrest?" Her voice was just as sweet and gentle as the charming little person herself.

"Yes, indeed, although you were already through with your daily lesson for today. Tama made an interesting suggestion to coordinate the different talents of the mutants. Over there is the salt lake; about six hundred feet from the shore, approximately over there where you can see that withered bush, a huge boulder of ten tons is resting at the bottom of the lake. Miss Ishi, what I would like you to do now is to estimate the depth of the water at that spot. Your friend Tama must have these figures if he is to complete his task. Do you get me?"

The young girl nodded. Then she smiled encouragement to her fellow Japanese and placed herself in such a way that her face was pointed directly at the spot indicated by Khrest. She closed her eyes, for if her gaze could penetrate solid objects, then her own eyelids did not present any obstacle to her vision. She concentrated deeply, her effort creasing deep furrows into her smooth forehead. Tama kept close to her, almost touching the slender figure. But his physical nearness did not seem to distract Ishi; quite the opposite. She stepped even closer to him and grasped his arm. She held it tight with both her tiny hands as if she needed his support. And then . . .

"I can see the rock!" Tama called out all of a sudden. He stood there, his eyes open wide, staring out to the lake. "I can see it now. The rock is lying on the ground among other rocks and rubble. The depth of the water is not more than sixty feet."

"Well done, Miss Ishi," Khrest complimented. "It is good to know that you can transmit your special ability. Tama, now will you start with your part of this task. Transform a tiny fraction of this rock into lead or gold, if you wish. Release some energy. But not too much; otherwise, the lake will start boiling."

Tama understood what Khrest wanted him to do. It was Khrest's duty to train the mutants. Perry Rhodan had given Khrest charge of his special corps, for Khrest was the only person capable of developing the mutants' talents to their full potential.

They all stood without moving. Five minutes. Ten minutes. A quarter of an hour.

Then, right above the spot where the boulder had disappeared below the water's surface, steam began to rise, slowly at first, then rapidly growing stronger. Air bubbles began to form, the water became agitated, sending small waves toward the shore, while other waves lost themselves along the watery expanse beyond the boiling whirlpool.

"That will do," Khrest said softly. "Tama, that's enough now. Tama, you can make the oceans boil if you so desire. I think we can conclude our lesson for today. By the way, Tama, what were you producing, gold or lead?"

Ishi opened her eyes and answered instead of Tama. "Gold, Mr. Khrest. Whoever finds this rock someday will be very glad. There are several pounds of gold sticking to that boulder."

Khrest was about to reply, when he was interrupted by a faint hum from his armband. He lifted his arm and pushed in a tiny knob. "Yes, Khrest speaking . . ."

It was Dr. Haggard, the medical specialist from Australia and discoverer of the antileukemia serum that had brought about Khrest's cure. He was calling from the *Stardust I.*

"Khrest, some unpleasant news. From Mercant. The M.S. are active again."

"I thought so. Where?"

"One case has been observed in the U.S. Their Secretary of Defense has fallen victim to the mind snatchers. Mercant managed to prevent the worst in the nick of time, but he is powerless in those cases that remain undetected. He would like to know if we could help him with it."

Khrest frowned. "Of course we will help him. Too bad though that Perry isn't back yet. Have you kept in communication with him?"

"Not since his last call from the Venus base. They must have left already in order to return to Earth."

"Establish contact with the *Good Hope.* Inform Rhodan of what you have told me. Maybe he will be able to locate the M.S. spaceship and destroy it. He has Tako Kakuta on board to help him, if necessary."

Tako Kakuta was a teleporter. Once already he had succeeded in transporting himself into one of the M.S. spacecraft and exploding it, with the help of a bomb he had teleported with him.

"I'll try to establish contact with Perry Rhodan in the *Good Hope*. But we should do something in the meantime."

Khrest looked over to Anne Sloane. "You are right. We can't wait. After all, that's what we have the mutant corps for. I am afraid our little troop will have to face its first trial. . . ."

The steaming jungles of Venus disappeared in the distance, and the planet itself became a gigantic silvery crescent whose brilliance surpassed even that of the near sun. This, of course, was an illusion. For the sun was in reality brighter even if smaller than Venus. However, the dense cloud cover reflected its light with such intensity that it became near impossible for the naked eye to look down on the second world of our solar system.

The tall, lean man standing in front of the picture screen did not move. Dreamily he regarded the receding planet that he was including in his plans from now on. Perry Rhodan had come to realize that Earth had become too small for him and that he needed a world of his own in order to build up his domain.

The eversilent Dr. Manoli sat close to Perry Rhodan. His slim body was hidden behind the back of his chair. Manoli, like Rhodan, devoted his attention to the planet that was now disappearing in the dark vastness of space. This planet so much resembled the way his own home planet, Earth, must have been one hundred million years ago.

Far less impressed by this awesome celestial spectacle was the third member of the crew inside the command center of the *Good Hope*. Reginald Bell's heavyset figure lay stretched out comfortably on his couch. The former engineer of the retired *Stardust I* was reading. His watery blue eyes skimmed rapidly over the pages of a book. His straight reddish hair seemed to stand on end, as if he were frightened by some horrible ghost story. Once in a while an ironic smile flitted across his broad features. He did not appear to be interested at all in the round globe of Venus, which seemed to shrink rapidly in size on the picture screen.

He was the first to break the silence in the cabin. He shook his head in disgust and placed his book on his round belly. Now the picture on the cover became visible. It showed a jungle landscape with a swamp. In the middle of the swamp a slender space rocket could be seen. It had sunk halfway down into the morass. A man was standing at the opened air lock, defending himself with a ray gun against some gruesome monster that looked like a dinosaur.

"What a guy! Such a thing should be illegal. His imagination is too wild. That isn't healthy!" Bell exclaimed loudly.

Perry Rhodan did not take his eyes off the screen. Without turning his head he inquired, "Whose imagination don't you approve of?"

"The author who wrote this novel."

"Which novel?"

Reginald Bell sighed deeply. "This science fiction novel, *Adventure on Venus*. Just imagine, the story was written more than twenty years ago. At that time nobody had any idea that we would be flying to Venus so soon. And that guy thinks up a story, has somebody construct a spaceship, fly to Venus, get stuck in the mud in a Venusian swamp and live there à la Robinson Crusoe. He battles heroically against dinosaurs and the sweltering heat until his friend arrives with a second space rocket and saves him. It's too incredible, Perry."

Perry Rhodan swung around his swivel chair and stared at his friend, lying there on the couch. He would never cease wondering at the harmless appearance of Reg. How deceptive his exterior was! For both friends were the human beings with the highest I.Q.s in all the universe. They owed this superior intelligence to the Arkonide hypnotraining, which had endowed them within a few days with an extensive and advanced state of knowledge that far surpassed the total sum of all Earthly intelligence. The scientific achievements of the age old Arkonide civilization were safely stored in the memory banks of the two men. Reg most certainly did not look the part of a genius; quite the contrary. Even Rhodan was occasionally tempted to underestimate his friend's potential when seeing his harmless face. Still, he knew what was hidden behind those watery blue eyes.

"What's so incredible about that? Wasn't that author right, after all? Don't we have such jungles and prehistoric monsters here on Venus? Isn't it hot?"

Reg sighed again. "That's just it! The guy is so right in what he describes. Venus is just the way he imagined it to be. I am ready to believe this guy must have been here on Venus before us." Bell sat up and rubbed his right elbow. "It's simply uncanny."

"Come on, Reg. You are a bit jealous of that writer. You shouldn't begrudge him his fabulous imagination, which let him experience vicariously twenty years ago what has come true today. He was ahead of his time, and you can't stand that."

"But the ray gun . . . what nonsense! Twenty years ago people did not even have the technical knowhow for such weapons."

"But we used such a ray gun only the day before yesterday to drive off one of the fat beasts that intended to gobble up our ship for a nice dinner."

Reg's face became distorted in a grimace of despair. "For crying out loud! *We* did not invent these ray guns!"

"So what's the difference, as long as we have them? What does it matter that the Arkonides supplied us with these ray guns? Without the Arkonides we wouldn't be here either, for they gave us the *Good Hope*, too."

Reg gave up the fight. "O.K., have it your way. No use quarreling. That writer was a genius, way ahead of his time, wrote immortal works, even surpassing reality. If only he had been wrong in his imagination and had described it as a world filled with dust clouds . . . ! But no, his description is so accurate! I am getting all riled up about this. We can't report anything new when we get back to Earth!"

"Why do you read that stuff if it upsets you so much?"

Reg had no answer to this question. He could not even attempt to think up a reply, for suddenly the air between the two friends began to scintillate for a fraction of a second. Then a man materialized out of thin air where nothing had been before. Tako Kakuta, the Japanese mutant, had once again been too lazy to walk over from his radio communication center down the hall.

The *Good Hope* was an auxiliary vessel attached to the giant Arkonide cruiser that had been destroyed on the moon by the combined forces of the planet Earth. Thora, the female commander of the research expedition, had been able to salvage the "lifeboat" from that catastrophe and had fled to Earth, where she found refuge at Perry Rhodan's base in the Gobi Desert. The auxiliary craft was tremendous measured by terrestrial standards. It had a diameter of over one hundred and eighty feet, was spherical, and could travel at faster than light speeds. The spacecraft could accelerate at any desired speed, since it was supplied with gravitation neutralizers that nullified the otherwise unbearable stress exerted on any living organism. The vessel was equipped with advanced types of weapons that surpassed all human imagination. The boat's effective range of five hundred light-years lay, according to Khrest, below the minimum needed by the Arkonides to return to their home planet, or even to reach the nearest base of their farflung galactic empire.

The radio communication center of the gigantic spaceship was so far ahead of what was known on Earth that Tako could comprehend only a small part of its machinery and installations. He merely made use of the small transmitter that produced normal radio waves. Thus he established radio communication with Earth. It would take several months before he would understand the structure and workings of the other instruments of the Arkonide supertechnology.

For a while the contact with the Gobi Desert base had been interrupted. The distance between Earth and Venus had become too great. But now they were rushing back to their home planet with such incredible speeds that soon they were able to hear Dr. Haggard's radio signals. They became so loud it was impossible not to hear them.

That was the reason why the Japanese teleported himself into the command center where Perry Rhodan and Reginald Bell were stationed.

Bell reacted to this surprise, as usual, by being half scared to death. There was really no excuse for that, but he could not help feeling shocked every time he saw Tako materialize in the empty air before him.

"Is that trip really necessary? Do you have to appear unannounced any time and anywhere?"

Tako smiled gently. "In the future I'll first teleport a letter to announce my impending arrival. Will that suit you better?"

Bell's reply was not fit to be printed.

Rhodan cut their banter short. "Did you get in touch with the Gobi base?"

"That's why I came to see you," replied a now very serious Tako. "Dr. Haggard had been calling for hours trying to reach us. Bad news, Mr. Rhodan. The M.S. invasion has begun. Mercant reported several cases where the M.S. have taken over the bodies of important personalities. It doesn't help though if they are found out, as Dr. Haggard said. The M.S. then simply withdraw and seek another host."

Bell pushed aside the book that had so greatly displeased him some seconds earlier. He sat up straight on his couch, his eyes suddenly filled with cold fury. "What did you say just now? Invasion? But we destroyed the ship of the intruders!"

"Then they must have more than one ship," remarked Rhodan, and turned to Manoli. "Let's forget about Venus now, Eric! Switch the picture over to Earth. As fast as possible!"

The picture on the viewing screens changed. A small greenish-blue globe became visible with a tiny dot near it, the moon. Both celestial bodies quickly grew in size while they were looking at them.

Rhodan addressed the young Japanese. "Was there anything else?"

"Khrest requests your immediate return to the Gobi Desert base. He wants to put the mutant corps into action. He sees no other possibility to proceed against the invasion. He would like to speak to you."

"Then let's go," decided Rhodan, and walked out of the room. Tako briefly grimaced at Bell; then he disappeared just as suddenly as he had come.

When Rhodan entered the communications center Tako was already waiting for him. He was calling Haggard. "Perry Rhodan wishes to talk to Khrest."

Rhodan waited for a few moments; then he acknowledged Khrest's voice, greeting him across space. "Khrest, this is Rhodan speaking. What's the trouble?"

"Listen, Rhodan, the situation is critical. Mercant is desperate. He has asked for help. I did not want to do anything without first consulting you. How soon can you be back here?"

"In about two to three hours. I hope the space sphere can take this."

"Don't worry, Rhodan. If you should sight the M.S. spaceship, don't hesitate to destroy it. Have Tako teleport himself into the enemy ship with some explosives."

"They will be more cautious this time, I am afraid. They have been warned by their first experience. They might have brought along some additional reinforcements."

"That's out of the question. The M.S. mentality forbids them to contact any other race to come to their assistance. They believe themselves to be superior to any creature in this universe and to be able to overcome any opponent. In my opinion it is almost impossible to conquer them completely."

"You underestimate us once again, Khrest. By the way, I have located a suitable place on Venus for us. We will establish our second base there and proceed with the training of our mutant corps."

"This project will have to wait until we have defeated the invaders. Mankind has no idea what's in store for them. I fear the M.S. must have established a beachhead on Earth from which they operate. It would be too cumbersome for them to use a moving spaceship as base of operations."

"Any idea where this base might be?"

"None whatsoever. You will have to talk to Mercant about this. He has spoken with several persons who had been invaded by the M.S. and then have been abandoned by them. He received some information from these people."

Rhodan was perplexed. "I thought anybody would die once they had been possessed by the M.S. Has anything changed there?"

"We were wrong in assuming this. The liberated victims showed no harmful aftereffects."

"Excellent. That's one thing to our advantage. Now, something else, Khrest—you realize that we must never lose the position we occupy in our relations with the world's big power blocs. They united only because of our presence, which they feared. Without this threat from the Third Power mankind will soon revert to the same chaotic conditions they have barely overcome. The old conflicts will split their newly found union apart. Therefore, I consider it vital to defeat the invaders as quickly as possible. This must have precedence over any other problems now. If we fail, we will forfeit everything we have gained. All our prestige will vanish overnight."

Rhodan could almost see the amused smile with which the Arkonide scientist answered, "Our prestige would not be the only thing to vanish in that case! So would all of mankind. And we would be lost too. The positronic brain predicts that we are in exactly such a crisis."

"And what are our chances? What does the positronic brain have to say to that?"

"At least fifty fifty."

Perry Rhodan thought for a while before he asked, "The *Good Hope* has a range of five hundred light-years. Couldn't we attack the home planet of the M.S. with it?"

Khrest sighed. "Your drive is rather frightening, Rhodan. So much energy! There might be a chance later on, but for the moment the prognosis is pretty hopeless. The M.S. avoid any direct confrontation, but they keep up their defense system. The *Good Hope* alone is not enough for an attack."

"That remains to be seen," said Rhodan, who did not abandon the idea entirely. "Will you get in touch with Mercant. I'll expect to see him or one of his men at the base when I return. Then we can map out our strategy. Is there anything else?"

"No, not for the time being. Thora is acting reasonable for a change."

"Well, she had better!" commented Rhodan with a shrug of his shoulders. "So long then, Khrest."

While Rhodan was walking back to the command center he seemed lost in thought. His mind was preoccupied with Thora, the commanding officer of the Arkonide expedition. What an unusual woman, even if she was afflicted with the morbid prejudice of racial superiority! The Earthlings were nothing but half savages in her eyes. Only under pressure had she declared her willingness to cooperate with Perry Rhodan. She realized that she was stranded here in this, to her, previously unknown solar system from which she could never find her way back home unless mankind would help her build a suitable spaceship. There was no hope that her own highly intelligent but utterly decadent race would lift a finger to search for her or even come to her rescue. Most likely no one would ever notice that the scientific research ship was missing.

Thora was a woman of captivating beauty. Perry could almost have loved her if he had not hated her even more. But was it really hatred he felt, or did he only imagine it? How good it was to have Khrest at his side, to explain the psychological reasons for Thora's incomprehensible behavior.

Rhodan shrugged and entered the center.

The picture screen in the middle showed Earth with clearly discernible continents. They would soon be landing.

Mercant had not come in person. The load of responsibility for the Western Bloc's security rested so heavily on his shoulders that he no longer left his underground fortress below the Greenland ice pack, from where he directed all actions.

One of his most capable employees was Captain Klein, who worked for the defense system. He was also Rhodan's ally. Mercant had nominated Klein as his personal liaison with Perry Rhodan.

Captain Klein was admitted through the momentarily lifted energy barrier. He was led to Perry Rhodan, who barely five hours earlier had still been on Venus. Khrest was sitting silently on a couch in the back of the room, together with Thora. Also present at this meeting were Bell and Manoli, Dr. Haggard and the telepath John Marshall, a member of the mutant corps.

Rhodan greeted Klein and encouraged him to speak. "Let's hear your report, Captain Klein! I presume that Mercant authorized you to speak on his behalf and gave you all available information regarding the situation. How bad is it?"

"Quite bad, even if we can't yet fully gauge the extent of the invasion that is proceeding in all secrecy. The

M.S. are clever, they keep learning from their initial mistakes. At first they were rather clumsy and could be easily detected. This was not much help, though, since an M.S. simply leaves his host's body, permitting the victim's mind to return unharmed, except that the latter cannot remember anything that went on during the interlude when his intellect was imprisoned in the M.S.'s own insect body. The M.S. can then pick a new target. They have by now reached such a degree of perfection that it has become almost impossible to detect them. But even if they should be found out, the M.S. cannot be rendered harmless unless their host is killed on the spot. We know of no way out of this terrible dilemma."

"*But I do*," insisted Rhodan. "I know the M.S. have established a base somewhere on this planet. This is where their bodies rest while their intellects change places with those of their victims. If we could find this base and then destroy their bodies we could succeed in killing off their intellects. For they are dependant on this link with their own bodies in order to survive. A rather complicated process for which we have undeniable proof."

Perry Rhodan fell silent. He could hear Thora's excited whispering in the background. She was apparently trying to talk Khrest into something. Her golden eyes were flashing with a dangerous fire. Was she making another attempt to incite her fellow Arkonide against the human race? Rhodan felt anger rise in him, but he suppressed it. The day would come when he would prove to this arrogant woman how much need she had of mankind.

"Go on, Captain Klein!" urged Rhodan. "What does Mercant propose to do about this?"

"Place all important personalities under strict surveillance to avoid any infiltration. That's all."

"Well, that is not too much," Perry Rhodan admitted. Khrest moved in the background. He stood up.

"Yes, Khrest, what is it?"

All eyes turned in the direction of the tall scientist, whose glance flickered strangely in a manner no one had ever observed in him before. His voice sounded a little shaky as he said, "Thora has been able to convince me that it is senseless to fight against the M.S. We have a lot of experience with them. So far they have conquered every solar system they ever discovered. If we had not surrounded our galactic empire with a dense ring of alarm systems, and if we had not destroyed every oval spaceship during its approach, there would no longer exist any Arkonide galactic realm. Nothing can stop the advance of the M.S."

Rhodan frowned. "So what? Why are you telling us all this? Has Thora encouraged you to do so?"

Khrest looked back to Thora; he seemed helpless. Quickly she came to his assistance. She jumped up and stood there like a goddess of vengeance with fiery golden eyes. Her pale hair had almost the same color as her delicate skin, which was barely beginning to show a tan from the strong desert sun. She was beautiful, of an un-Earthly beauty!

"Yes, I have encouraged him, Perry Rhodan. You are aware just as well as I myself that Khrest has been weakened by his long illness. And his mind in particular has been affected by it. If we are going to remain here on Earth to fight a hopeless battle against the M.S., we will waste our last remaining shred of strength. I have suggested to Khrest that we should leave this solar system and search for another one that has not yet been discovered by the M.S. Khrest has agreed to my proposal. Our decision is irrevocable."

Rhodan warned Bell with a stern look. His impulsive friend was just about to advance threateningly in Thora's direction.

"So you want to leave our planet in a lurch," Rhodan said in a matter of fact voice. "The same planet that came to your rescue when you needed help."

"Who helped whom?" demanded Thora.

"The help was mutual. May I remind you that Khrest would no longer be alive without Dr. Haggard's medical skill and Earthly medical knowhow."

"And if it had not been for you my crew would still be alive. But you killed them during the treacherous surprise attack on the moon. We are quits!"

"Not by far! But I want to ask you something else. Please answer me honestly. Do the M.S. rank higher in the galactic classification than the Arkonides? Are they considered a superior race to your own?"

Thora's face became flushed with anger. "How dare

you even ask such a question! That insect race belongs to a primitive level, not worthy to inhabit the universe."

"But you are still ready to turn tail when they threaten here?" Rhodan said ironically. "Isn't that amazing? Doesn't that hurt your pride?"

"We are forced by necessity. Here we don't have the weapons we need to defeat the M.S."

"How about trying this without these weapons? We can invent new ones that might be even better. Mankind is not willing to accept the M.S. invasion as an immutable fact. We will defend ourselves and chase them off. And you, Thora, are going to help us with that."

"You can't force me to do so."

"I am not so sure about that," countered Rhodan with studied deliberateness. "I have a way of forcing you. Without the *Good Hope* you are powerless, Thora. From now on neither you nor any of your robots will be admitted to the *Good Hope*. You are not to leave your quarters inside the base."

"You place me under house arrest?" shouted Thora, full of fury. "You wouldn't dare!"

"I am simply taking all necessary measures to ward off the M.S. invasion. Khrest said once that the Earthlings resemble the very early Arkonides in this respect. He is right. We are hard and determined to reach our goal. My goal now is to deal a crushing blow to the M.S. from which they can never recover. I want to find a weapon against them that someday will also be of use to your own nation. But you, Thora, will under no circumstances stand in my way! And neither are you going to desert with the *Good Hope*. Have I made myself clear?"

Thora regarded him with hatred in her eyes—but there was something else besides hatred hidden in them. Rhodan was seized by a piquant thrill recognizing the significance of the sensation that was slowly rising from the unconscious mind of the woman opposite him. It was admiration and a bit of surrender—or even beginning love.

Rhodan was confused, but he did not show it. There would be plenty of time later to analyze this paradox. Right now there were more urgent matters to attend to. Little did he know that at that moment Khrest came to a decision too. The scientific leader of the Arkonide expedition, who had met many races of the universe and had dealings with all kinds of peoples within the Arkonide empire, realized suddenly with absolute certainty that the human race was the one to become the heirs of this galactic empire. He felt no regret when he recognized this fact, which he then proceeded to register and store in his immense brain.

Captain Klein interrupted the silence. "Lieutenant Li Tschai-tung, our ally from the Asiatic Federation, has disappeared. Mercant believes that the M.S. got hold of him."

This unexpected shock jolted even Perry Rhodan.

Lieutenant Li was one of the leading agents of the Asiatic Federation. At the time he was put into action against Rhodan, he was one of the first men to realize that the big powers had to unite if they wanted to stand up against the might of the Arkonides. But once this unity had been brought about he had understood Rhodan's motivations and learned to appreciate highly the former test pilot of the Western Bloc. Together with his colleagues Kosnow from the Eastern Bloc and Klein from the Western Bloc he had gone over to the side of the Third Power. Klein became the liaison between Rhodan and Mercant, while Li became the link between Rhodan and the secret service of the Asiatic Federation.

And now the M.S. appeared to have overpowered this man. Thus, Rhodan was attacked directly for the first time, apart from some insignificant episodes during their first attempt.

"What do you mean by that—'he disappeared'? Li can't have disappeared into a void."

"Li disappeared from Greenland and returned to China without being authorized to do so. Mercant thinks that the M.S. intend to undermine and ruin the big powers one by one."

"Why would they pick on our liaison officers for that purpose?" Rhodan regarded Klein with some uneasiness.

The captain noticed the feelings of distrust that were rising in Rhodan. He shook his head. "If you should be thinking the M.S. have got hold of me, too, then I must disappoint you. Is there no way you can ascertain the presence of an M.S.?"

"How do you propose one could go about that?"

"I have no idea; but I thought that you with your technical means—"

"The frequency detector!" Bell interjected nonchalantly.

Rhodan acknowledged the suggestion with an angry slap on his thigh. He was annoyed at himself for not having thought of this right away. Of course—that was a possibility. The highly sensitive detector set could receive the vibrations of the human brain and register their frequencies. The detector was capable of distinguishing between a normal brain and that of a mutant, despite the fact that the difference was rather slight between the two sets of brainwaves. How tremendous, on the other hand, must be the difference between the human brain and that of the insectlike M.S.!

"You are right, Reg! That should give us an efficient method of determining whether somebody has been taken over by the M.S. The only question remaining is what to do in such a case. We can't simply kill that person, if there is any chance left of saving his life. There is no sense in chasing the M.S. from one human body to another."

From the background came Khrest's voice, which could be heard over Thora's protestations. "The thing to do is to destroy the body of the M.S. that he left behind sleeping somewhere. This in turn will cause the human mind, imprisoned in the insect's own body, to return to his own. The mind of the M.S., on the other hand must die together with his own body. That is their only known vulnerable spot; we must exploit this weakness."

"How do you suggest going about tracking down the M.S. mind on its way back to its body?"

Khrest smiled enigmatically. "This is something you will have to learn by experience. This is where the mutants will have to come in. Perhaps they might succeed in bridging the gap between the M.S. mind and body."

"Maybe," agreed Rhodan half heartedly. He considered it unlikely that they could ever trace a nonmaterial substance moving at the speed of light. Mind was a form of energy, and thus undoubtedly a form of matter. It was possible to detect it, but he was not so sure about pursuing it. Or could there be some chance . . . ?

Klein used the lull in conversation to remark, "Mercant

asks you, Mr. Rhodan, to track down Li. He can't manage this task by himself. Li is liable to cause great damage. Mercant is of the opinion that the M.S. will try to shatter the world's newly found unity. A divided enemy will be an easier target for the M.S. That absolutely must not happen."

"You say Li has gone to China?"

"Yes. That is as far as we could trail him; then we lost sight of him. We are inclined to believe that he is now in Peking."

Rhodan turned to Bell. "Get me Ernst Ellert, but quick!"

Reginald Bell left without comment. Only Khrest's whitish eyebrows arched upward in surprise.

"What is Ellert supposed to do?"

Since Klein had never heard about Ellert's special talents, Rhodan saw fit to give forth with an explanation. "Ernst Ellert is a mutant. His abilities surpass anything that the human mind could conceive so far. He is a teletemporarian. That means that he is capable of sending his mind ahead into the future and thus looking back on the past of our present time. Maybe he will succeed in hunting down the secret hiding place of the M.S."

"Teletemporarian?" murmured Klein, who was obviously at a loss to understand Rhodan's explanation. Then he shrugged and kept silent. He trusted Perry Rhodan to know what needed to be done.

Ellert arrived, and at first sight it was difficult for those who had been told about his unusual gifts to suppress a certain disappointment. The German looked perfectly normal, showing no indication of any special ability. However, his eyes burned with a steady, never flagging fire. These eyes had peered into eternity, Rhodan thought whenever he looked at them.

"We are holding a council of war," Perry Rhodan told Ellert. "The M.S. have started their invasion of Earth. Lieutenant Li, special agent of the Asiatic Defense System, has been taken over by them. Tako Kakuta will give you all necessary information. He will also accompany you. I hope you will be successful. Before you leave I will give you two frequency detectors and further instructions."

Rhodan hesitated for a moment before he continued. He had to exert a special effort to bring himself to say what was on his mind. "I felt reluctant so far to make use of your special talents, Mr. Ellert. Will you permit me a private question? You have lived in the future more than once. That means you sent your mind ahead, while your body remained in the present time. By the way, the fact that you can leave your body at will and then let your mind slip back into it puts you on the same level as the M.S. However, you surpass them by far, since your intellect is not chained to our present time. Can you understand now why I have chosen to put you into action against the M.S.? If ever there was anybody who could represent a real danger to them, it is you! But back again to my original question. You were often in the future, Ellert. Have you ever found any indications there that the Third Power will exist in the future? Will we defeat the invaders?"

A shadow flitted across Ellert's face. "I am sorry to have to disappoint you. No, not in that sense. Don't jump to any conclusions yet! But the future is nothing concrete. Many ways lead into the future, or let me say, rather, there is not just *one* future. Our present time is something real that has evolved out of a past that by now has become a fixed reality. But the future is unreal and uncertain. The smallest event taking place in the present time can change it. Therefore, I have never yet been in a future that could not still have been changed. Do you follow me?"

Rhodan slowly nodded to confirm that he did comprehend. Ellert continued, "There are thousands of potential futures, futures with and without Perry Rhodan. Yet only *one* of all these possible futures will become reality. I know that you must feel disappointed now, but my gift to be able to travel ahead in time, even if only with my mind, is without any practical value for you. I could slip into the wrong time stream and then my report would not be true."

"Why is it that you know all that and have never before discussed it with me?" asked Rhodan with a hint of reproach in his voice.

"I did not know it myself," Ellert admitted, embarrassed. "I did some experiments in the last few days and had to learn that different worlds exist simultaneously. But only one of those will later turn into reality. I have no clues which it will be."

"I see. Then you are totally useless to us as a prophet."

Ellert made a gesture expressing regret. However the knowing fire still remained in his eyes. Was he not speaking the truth? Rhodan looked questioning toward John Marshall. But the telepath slowly shook his head. So Ellert was not lying. He spoke the truth. What then was it that gave him this knowing look?

"You might be useless to us as a prophet," Rhodan continued, "but not as an opponent against the invaders. You are capable of leaving your body to try to pursue the M.S."

"I'll try to do my best, together with Tako, to solve the task you have set for me," promised Ellert. Then, after some hesitation, he added, "According to one of the many potential futures I will not be among the living in a few weeks. But as I mentioned already, this is just *one* possibility among many. This one has just as much chance of coming true as another where I will assist you way ahead in a far future to consolidate the existence of the great galactic empire."

Perry Rhodan did not reply. He was very pensive as both Ellert and Tako Kakuta, the Japanese teleporter, left the conference room.

CHAPTER THREE

Another conference room.

More than six thousand feet below the Greenland ice cap the three presidents of the big powers met for the first time—not, as before, in order to hatch plots against Rhodan. This time they were searching for an effective way to beat back the invaders. Mercant was present. Perry Rhodan participated in the meeting via a television installation. The narrow end wall was covered by a huge television screen. Rhodan's life size figure could be seen on it. All members of the little group in the conference room could see and hear Rhodan the same way that he could perceive them. Nothing indicated that they were separated by thousands of miles.

Mercant opened the meeting and then called upon Perry Rhodan to explain the strategic situation.

"Gentlemen!" Rhodan came to the point immediately.

"Unless we proceed to act at once we are lost. Fortunately for mankind a union of our world has been accomplished, and thus Earth can finally be called Terra. All frontiers have practically been removed. You, gentlemen, are ruling the world, apart from myself, representing the Third Power and the might of the Arkonides. Also, in the field of economics, our efforts are being coordinated.

"I request that my agents and all authorized personnel may move unhindered in your countries. They must have free access to all government offices and especially to those of your defense systems. My people have been ordered to place all important personalities of the world under strict surveillance in order to become aware at once if any of them have been invaded by the M.S. For this purpose I need unrestricted power of attorney. I must request you to give me complete authority."

An embarrassed silence ensued. No one dared refuse Rhodan's demand; yet . . .

Mercant intervened. "There is no doubt that you gentlemen appreciate the necessity of this unusual procedure and will make your arrangements accordingly. This is what you intended to do, isn't it?"

The President of the Western Bloc nodded consent. Reluctantly, the President of the Asiatic Federation and the President of the Eastern Bloc followed suit. They saw no other way out of the dangerous situation they were faced with.

Rhodan breathed a sigh of relief. He had won the first round. "Thank you, gentlemen! This, then, takes care of the defense measures to be taken against the invading forces, as far as you are concerned. You no longer need worry about it. I am confident of accomplishing whatever is necessary with the help of my own forces. As soon as we locate the enemy spacecraft, we will destroy it as we did their first ship. But let's discuss now the second point on our agenda. As you all know I have founded an organization, the General Cosmic Company. The manager of this trust concern is Homer G. Adams, the well-known financial genius with the eidetic memory. Our industrial installations have sprung up everywhere on Earth. We dispose of a working capital in excess of thirty-five billions. If you are willing to cooperate also in this area with me officially, I am ready on my part to advance the sum of thirty billions for a project we are planning for all of us."

The President of the Asiatic Federation leaned forward. "What project are you referring to?" he inquired eagerly.

Perry Rhodan smiled. "A space fleet! Our planet must have a space fleet!"

"What for?"

"There are many reasons, Mr. President. One of these is purely economic. It is no longer a secret that war and military rearmament used to be a part of the economic welfare of a state. This may sound rather cynical, but is nevertheless a sober fact. We must therefore proceed according to this well proved principle. With this exception, though—our efforts will no more serve to manufacture arms for war, but we will have a new goal, to build a space fleet. This will bring about an economic boom for all nations on Earth. New industries will arise, every able person will find work. We will stamp factories and huge industrial enterprises out of the ground. We will find new methods of producing new materials and manufacturing thus far unknown machines.

"I have spoken about the purely economic aspect and the tremendous advantages for all of mankind. But there is also a military reason for having a space fleet. You destroyed the Arkonide explorer cruiser on the moon. An emergency signal was released automatically when this happened. This S.O.S. is broadcast by radio waves with faster than light speeds throughout the universe. These signals are intercepted by space traveling races. The current invasion is a result of this. But other races might be curious too and seek us out. Terra must be ready to ward off any further invasions. For this purpose we need a space fleet. I hope that you will see the logic of my reasoning and agree with me."

All present agreed, and Rhodan's proposal was accepted unanimously. But Rhodan was not yet through. His next request concerned the ways and means for forming a united government of the world. Rhodan concluded his motion with these words: "Once and for all we must have the guarantee that no more divisions of power will occur among the nations of the world. The building of the space fleet will contribute to enduring unity. But we must take care in other ways to nurture this feeling of belonging to one larger entity, going beyond the national frontiers. The United States of the World must become a reality, this age old dream of utopians that has been ridiculed so long. Never has there been such a favorable prognosis for this federation of all men as today. The common danger we face and the common efforts we will have to make to build the space fleet will act as inspiration for all of us. Will you please, as soon as possible, begin all necessary negotiations. That is all I have to tell you, gentlemen. Please proceed now on your own. I am not interested in the internal problems. Mercant will keep me informed of all the essentials. Thanks for your confidence in me; you will never have to regret it."

The television screen on the wall grew dark.

All remained silent until Mercant remarked, "Our goals have been determined, gentlemen. It is up to you whether we reach them. I wanted to make sure that we would get some tangible results out of today's meeting, and I have therefore asked someone to join us here. This man will be able to advise us in all financial and economical matters. Gentlemen, may I present Homer G. Adams, manager of the G.C.C."

Ernst Ellert and Tako Kakuta were holding a council of war in their hotel room in Peking.

"You must be able to do it," urged Ellert. "Just remember how you exploded the oval shaped M.S. spaceship. You teleported yourself, together with the bomb, into the enemy's ship. If you could transport a bomb with you then you should also be able to carry along a human being. You have proved that you can teleport any matter that you touch. Also, Ishi Matsu can transfer onto others her ability to see through matter, even when it is far removed."

"You might be right," admitted the Japanese with a polite smile. "We would have to carry out such an experiment. I have never thought of such a possibility. It simply never occurred to me till now, to be truthful."

"We must experiment to find out all about our potential. This goes for the rest of the mutant corps. It will take many years of experience to stabilize our forces."

"How about taking me along into the future?" asked the

Japanese in all earnestness. "We should reciprocate favors!"

Ellert grinned impishly. "Is that how you imagine our much praised consolidation of forces to function?" he mocked, "If Khrest had any idea of this . . ."

Tako turned serious again. They had had their fun; now back to their task. "We have found Li," he stated. "What are we going to do with him now? How can we know if he is going to do some foolish things, maybe even dangerous ones? We can't warn the government offices of the Asiatic Federation. Who can be sure how many of them have already been taken over by the M.S.?"

He had hardly finished when the buzzers of both their all purpose sets began to sound. They pushed the receiver button and heard the voice of Ras Tschubai, the second teleporter of Rhodan's mutant corps.

"Listen, there is some work for you. Li just drove to the airport and bought a ticket for the stratoliner to Batang. The plane leaves tomorrow morning at six thirty-five."

"What a ghastly time to have to get up!" moaned Ellert, who loved to sleep late. "What does Li want in Batang, of all places?"

"How should I know? He did not state a reason for his trip when he bought the ticket."

"You have a point there," laughed Ellert. "Why don't you come to join us here? Li won't get away during the night. When is he due to arrive in Batang?"

"The flight lasts two hours. At about eight thirty, I should think."

"We will meet him with a reception committee in Batang," said Ellert. "Okay, don't worry any more about Li. Just jump!"

It took only one second for the heavyset African to materialize in the middle of the hotel room. He broke out in a grin when he saw that Ellert and Kakuta were startled at his sudden appearance. They jumped quite unconsciously, for no one can get used to seeing a person appear out of the void—not even another teleporter.

"Do you have any idea what our friend wants in Tibet, of all places?" Tako asked. "Batang lies in direction of Tibet, if I am not mistaken."

"You are not," confirmed Ras. "More than a thousand miles. Quite some jump, I must say. How will we do that?"

"We'll take Ellert between us, and then we'll jump. Let's hope we can make it."

Ras's eyes grew to saucer size. "Take Ellert between us, in the middle? Do you mean to say that we will take him along when we jump?"

"Why not?" asked Tako. "He isn't as heavy as a medium sized bomb! So what about it?"

The plane landed at the scheduled time. Li disembarked and walked to the airport buildings without looking right or left. He seemed to feel absolutely safe. Since a Japanese would not be conspicuous here at Batang, Tako had taken charge of Li's direct surveillance. He kept in constant touch with his two colleagues by way of his tiny transmitter, concealed in a bracelet.

Li had no luggage, but he carried a large sum of cash. How he had obtained the money, no one knew, least of all probably Li himself. He took a room in one of the most expensive hotels, paid three days' rent in advance, and then did not leave his room for the rest of the morning. Tako kept watch sitting in a little bar across from the hotel. He was utterly bored. He was afraid of falling asleep and hoped to be relieved from this dull duty as soon as possible.

Ras came to Tako's rescue toward noon. He ordered a drink and assured his Japanese friend that he would not at all mind staying in the little bar till evening. Not quite so sure about that and a bit unsteady on his legs, Tako left the bar and went straight to the hotel, where he was awaited by Ellert.

"What on Earth do you think Li wants to do in this godforsaken town?" asked Ellert. He had been lying on his bed reading a book when Tako entered the room in a most conventional manner. Now he put his book aside and asked the question that had preoccupied him all morning.

Tako was just as puzzled about Li's reason for being in Batang. "I haven't the faintest idea," he sighed, and flopped into the nearest chair. "We couldn't very well ask him personally. But couldn't you peek into the future and find out what his intentions are?"

"I have no way of knowing whether I will reach the real future or simply some probability time stream. Fortunately, my mind is not tied to my body. It can move freely about, not being bound to any matter. I can travel even at right angles to the time stream, if necessary. But I never know whether what I am seeing will eventually happen."

"Why don't you give it a try!" suggested Tako, who had only a vague notion about teletemporation. "I'll keep watch on your sleeping body here."

Ellert nodded and remained lying on his bed. "There won't be any harm in doing it," he admitted. "But I can't tell how long this trip will take. Don't let anybody enter this room. Make sure of that!"

Tako stood up and walked over to lock the door. When he came back to the bed, Ellert was lying there already motionless with closed eyes. Tako bent over his friend and stopped short. Ellert had stopped breathing—or was this only a delusion? His pulse was weak. Tako pinched Ellert's cheek, but there was no response.

Tako decided to take a nap, since there was nothing much he could do now. His head had hardly hit the pillow before he was asleep. Nothing disturbed this peaceful afternoon.

In the meantime Li was sitting in his hotel room a few blocks away. The intellect that had invaded his brain, thereby replacing Li's own intellect, had established telepathic communication with its commanding officer high up in space, traveling in an oval shaped spaceship.

"We will have to abandon our plan to protect our base on the third planet. The human being by the name of Li has become suspect. But it would be senseless to try to take over another human body. We would have to start all over again. Besides, Li has only aroused suspicion; no one is certain about his state. Li will remain in Batang for two more days; then he will fly to the United States. Wait for further instructions."

From that moment on Li's activities had no rhyme or reason. He wandered aimlessly around town, seeming to ignore the people that were shadowing him. On the third day he bought a ticket to Carson City, Nevada, by way of Hong Kong.

Just as was to be expected, Ellert's attempt had remained unsuccessful. On the contrary, everyone was still more confused. Ellert had left the present time and had advanced

51

into the future. His disembodied mind had floated above Li as he was flying from Hong Kong to Nevada. A horizontal shift in the time stream had shown another possibility. The same airplane, but without Li sitting in it. How could one tell which was the truth?

It began to dawn on Ellert how little practical use could be made of his extraordinary ability. Each point in present time was a pivot that led into all potential futures. There was an infinite number of different directions events could take. Only the present could determine the *one* path that would come true. Looking ahead into the future could only reveal all the various potential ways, but no one knew which of all these possibilities would become reality.

Therefore, any event that had ever happened could never be changed again. Time could not be turned back for retroactive changes.

While Ellert was mulling over these thoughts another idea had occurred to him. He was not yet capable of appreciating its full extent. He must discuss this with Perry Rhodan. If his theory should prove correct, then the days of the M.S. on Earth were numbered. . . .

Perry Rhodan and Ellert were sitting alone and undisturbed in the command center of the old *Stardust I*. This was Rhodan's favorite retreat, where he felt most at ease. This was where his fantastic career had started.

Ellert began with his report. "We did not follow Li during his flight to the U.S.; we knew his destination. In the meantime John Marshall seems to have taken him under his wing. And according to what I was told, Anne Sloane is also staying in Carson City. I must agree to your notion that Nevada Fields must be Li's next stop."

"This would make most sense," Rhodan confirmed calmly.

"While I had left my body in order to observe Li in the future I made a remarkable discovery. The M.S. communicate with each other telepathically! I even managed to understand part of their conversations. Unhindered by our material hull, our body, our intellect works in a more perfect and advanced way. If need be, we could probably communicate directly with the M.S. via telepathy. But this would make no sense in my opinion. For it is much better if they never find out about this possibility. Another idea that came to me—I am convinced that it is possible to pursue a disembodied M.S. mind. Any teleporter should be able to do so. A teleporter travels by transporting his body and mind together into another dimension and later materializes at a different place. In this respect he is nothing but pure spirit, somehow related to that of the M.S. Under these circumstances it seems quite likely that Ras or Tako, or even myself, can attach himself to the M.S. when the M.S. leaves a human body in order to return to his own insect hull."

Perry Rhodan had been listening very attentively. His brilliant brain considered the possibilities, evaluated the chances, and registered everything like an electronic robot. Therein he was assisted by the tremendous knowledge of the Arkonides. His memory banks discharged the needed information.

He looked up and said to Ellert, sitting across the small table, "You are right, Ellert. You are absolutely right. We will try it; we will take that risk. We believe that Li flew to Nevada with some special mission. Miss Sloane will keep me informed about Li's every move. But there is something else I want to discuss with you. You know that I never have made any demands on your talent as a teletemporarian. At first I refrained from doing so because of ethical reasons. In the meantime we have found out that the presence of the manyfold planes of probability forestall any attempt to obtain a clear vision of future events. Despite all this I must ask you to make an exception. Something very odd has taken place. . . ."

Ellert bent forward with great interest to view the newspaper article that Rhodan was pointing out to him. Huge headlines attracted his attention, and he began to read.

SIX YEAR OLD SHOOTS FATHER WITH HIS OWN GUN
Mysterious murder committed by a child.

Mesilla, New Mexico, from our special correspondent.

One of the most mysterious murders of the century happened yesterday morning in Mesilla, New Mexico.

Betty Toufry, a six year old girl, grabbed her father's gun, while sitting on his lap, and shot him. The child had never before handled the weapon and had no idea how to use it. . . .

Allan G. Toufry, the girl's father, as the article pointed out, had been an atomic scientist. He had been instrumental in the development of the latest type of atom bombs. He had been in charge of the most recent atom bomb tests in the desert. According to the report, the little girl had just minutes earlier run eagerly to greet her father. As he was embracing her, she had suddenly seemed startled. While she was seated on her father's lap the gun appeared to fly toward her hand. This scene was witnessed by the family maid, whose eyewitness report should be regarded with reservation, since the woman seemed to be in a highly hysterical state. In any case, continued the report, the case should be investigated thoroughly by psychological experts.

Ellert looked up to peer into Rhodan's questioning eyes.

"How does this strike you?" asked Perry.

Ellert shrugged. "Incredible! I am particularly intrigued by the family maid's statement. I am inclined to believe she was speaking the truth."

"So do I," admitted Rhodan. "I have a hunch, but I'd like to be on safe ground. Therefore, I would like you to find out what will happen to this child in the future. Especially what kind of person she will grow up to be. Can you find out for me?"

"Up to a certain point. Whichever direction the future will take eventually has no effect on the personality. That remains always the same regardless. It does not matter into which of the many potential futures I land; the main point is that Betty Toufry is alive now."

"That's what I thought, Ellert. Will you have to travel to New Mexico, or can you manage from here?"

"It would be more advantageous if I could be there. Besides, it would be close to Carson City."

"Okay, Ellert. That makes sense. Leave at once. Keep me informed. I am most interested in this little girl."

The telepaths were capable of immediately spotting the M.S. because of the aliens' peculiar thought pattern. The ring tightened closer and closer around the invaders but not without danger to their pursuers.

Nevada Spaceport was the main installation for the exploration of space. A tight cordon was placed around the whole area in order to keep out trespassers. Unfortunately, this did not affect the M.S.; they could cross the security zone at any time and then find a safe hiding place in their victims' bodies.

It was therefore essential for Rhodan's agents to keep watch on the inside of the cordoned off area and to be on the lookout for possible intruders.

This did not especially please Captain Burners from the Security Forces, but he did not have much choice in the matter. After all he had to obey the orders of his chief, Allan D. Mercant. He did not always understand these orders, lately, for he had been used to clear rules. Anyone who had no legitimate business inside the zone was not allowed to enter. That was plain enough. And now, all of a sudden, all kinds of strangers were permitted to stick their noses into matters that did not concern them in the least.

There was that Marshall, for instance. He was most exasperating. Kept smiling all the time as if he knew everything. What could that guy know, after all! Well, he was one of Rhodan's men, and Rhodan was supposed to have his fingers in every pie.

John Marshall, the telepath from Australia who had foiled a bank robbery by reading the criminal's mind, was now in Rhodan's service. Marshall was authorized to move freely wherever he liked inside Nevada Spaceport. It was only natural for him to make good use of this opportunity and to familiarize himself thoroughly with the farflung installations of the spaceport. He knew General Pounder, Chief of the Space Exploration Command, as well as his assistant, Colonel Maurice. He was friendly with Dr. Fleeps, of the Department of Space Medicine, the same as with Dr. Lehmann, the scientific director of the California Academy of Space Flight. And of course, he was also acquainted with Captain Burners.

So far Marshall had been unable to detect a single M.S. It seemed most improbable but was nevertheless the case. John racked his brain whether this was by accident or design, but could not find an answer. He kept all important personnel under constant surveillance and spoke with them every day, all the while exploring their thoughts, thanks to his mind reading abilities. Yet he could not discover anything suspicious.

Today he had been invited by Dr. Lehmann for a game of chess. The elderly gentleman was a passionate player and was happy to have found his match in the person of John Marshall. It goes without saying that the scientist had not the faintest notion how Marshall managed to be such an excellent chess player—he simply read the old man's mind and thus knew in advance every one of his moves.

"Check!" he said triumphantly, and moved his queen, believing he had won the game. With evident enjoyment he was puffing at his pipe, which gave off clouds of evil smelling smoke.

"Are you sure, Dr. Lehmann?" inquired the Australian. "Do you think I forgot about my bishop? You are wrong there. Well, what do you have to say now?"

Lehmann stared at the bishop, completely nonplussed. Indeed he had assumed that his partner in the game had forgotten all about the bishop that had been standing in a corner, completely hemmed in for the last ten minutes.

John lit a cigarette while Lehmann seized his queen between nicotine stained fingers. He raised the figure pensively. But in midair, Lehmann suddenly stopped moving. He seemed to turn to stone.

John, who was secretly amused at his opponent's intention to threaten his bishop by a stealthy move of his queen, suddenly realized with a start that Lehmann's thoughts had broken off abruptly.

He glanced at Lehmann, who was now sitting motionless like a stone figure. His eyes had assumed a vacant stare. His hand, still holding the queen, hovered above the chessboard. Not the slightest tremor could be noticed, not even a faint involuntary twitching of his eyelids.

At the same time John felt something pushing into the space that, an instant before, had been occupied by the professor's mind. With lightning speed John withdrew the tentacles of his own probing, telepathic mind from within Lehmann's brain. He kept only in loose touch so as not to disturb the penetrating alien mind of the M.S.

Marshall endeavored not to incur any suspicion. He knew that within a few seconds one of the invaders would look at him from Lehmann's eyes. This should take about five seconds, according to Mercant.

Indeed! When the five seconds had elapsed Lehmann began to stir. Like a puppet he put down the queen on a square where it made no sense at all. Life returned to his staring eyes. He looked questioningly at Marshall.

"Well?"

John tried to pull himself together. Never in his life before had he been faced with such an infernal situation. If only he could have penetrated into the alien's mind! But that was not as simple as that. The M.S. possessed some rudimentary traces of telepathic ability. He would become aware of his probing at once. Better not risk that.

"Not a smart move, Professor! It would mean checkmate for you. I'm sure you did not intend to do that really. I'll give you another chance." With these words Marshall seized his bishop and placed it in a rather unfavorable position. It should have been a simple matter for Lehmann to take advantage of John's gross negligence. But he did nothing of the sort. Apparently it took a certain time before the M.S. could appropriate all the information stored in his victim's memory banks. Lehmann's next move was nonsense and against all the rules of the chess game.

John pretended not to notice, and he in turn made a move that was not any less clumsy. While doing so he tried to approach the alien mind, but he ran into a mental obstacle that he could not overcome. He wanted to avoid applying force, lest he draw the opponent's attention to himself. This then meant that the M.S. were capable of screening off their own thoughts by placing a barrier around them. Thus it would be impossible to learn their intentions by reading their minds. There might nevertheless be a chance that the barrier would loosen up when the M.S. took up telepathic communication with each other. John must be sure to watch out for such a possibility.

The chess game proceeded in a most unorthodox manner, although the M.S. seemed to catch on fairly fast. John deemed it wise to let him win the game. Then he took his leave with a few harmless words. He concluded with: "I hope you'll keep your promise, Professor!"

"What promise?"

"The experiment. You haven't forgotten, surely. You suggested I should watch your next experiment with the newest combustion chamber. You wanted to test it in a couple of days."

"Oh . . . of course. You can come with me."

"Thank you, Professor. Good night."

"Good night."

Back in his room, Marshall took out the tiny but powerful transmitter from his suitcase. A few minutes later he was talking to Perry Rhodan, who was not pleased at first to be taken away from his early morning work with Khrest and the mutants.

As soon as he heard John's voice, all his anger vanished. He listened attentively to Marshall's report. Then he said slowly, "Keep Lehmann under strict surveillance. I have heard from Anne Sloane. Li is on his way to the Nevada Spaceport. He is supposed to be traveling on Mercant's orders. He intends to meet with Lehmann. It is probable that the two plan to carry out some secret mission that will paralyze our space exploration program. Be constantly on the alert! Get in touch with Miss Sloane as soon as she arrives. The moment Ellert completes his current assignment he will join you in your efforts. It looks as if Nevada Spaceport will soon become the turning point in the invasion."

Rhodan could not know how justified he was in that assumption.

It was not difficult for Ellert to trail Betty Toufry's path through the time stream. Five years in the future, he could recognize the best way of exploring her personality. All the parallel worlds coincided in a strange manner.

While he was floating invisibly above the young girl and penetrating her mind, he experienced a shocking surprise—Betty Toufry was a telepath!

She turned her head a little as if to listen; then a discreet smile flitted across her delicate features. She was sitting on the porch of the same house in which she had lived five years earlier with her father, when an unexpected event took place.

"Who are you?" she inquired soundlessly with her thoughts. Ellert could understand her clearly. He decided to drop any pretense. There was no sense in attempting to deceive her; he felt that her telepathic powers were superior to his own.

"I am Ernst Ellert, one of Perry Rhodan's collaborators."

"Well?" She appeared surprised. "Did Rhodan send you?"

Ellert was astonished at that reaction. "What do you mean by that?"

She seemed to reflect for a few moments. Then a little smile brightened her face. "I'm sorry, Ernst. I almost forgot. You have already told me five years ago about this visit you would pay me in the future. It was thanks to this meeting that Perry Rhodan decided five years ago to take me under his wing. Since that time I have been working with the mutant corps. Do you understand that?"

"Only partially," admitted the confused Ellert. "So you are working for Perry Rhodan; is that so?"

"Yes, indeed." She hesitated awhile before she continued, "Listen, Ernst! I am a mutant. My specialties are telekinesis and telepathy. At the age of six I already had an I.Q. twice that of a normal adult. New mutants are being born in all parts of the world. The new type of man is coming into being gradually and so far unnoticed. Someday we will totally replace *Homo sapiens.*"

"What a horrible vision!"

"Why? Do you regret that one stage of development will come to an end? I can't agree with you. Not *Homo sapiens* but *Homo superior* will become heir to the galactic empire."

Ellert's confusion grew constantly. This little girl, whose intellect surpassed by far his own, spoke of things that were talked about only in whispers in Rhodan's camp. Well, he had almost forgotten that he was five years in the future now. And most likely in the dimension of reality.

"Would you answer a question, Betty?"

"Yes, gladly."

"Why did you shoot your father five years ago?"

She seemed to hold back her thoughts at first, but then they came clearly. "As long as I can remember I would always read his thoughts. My mother had died when I was born. All my love was concentrated on him alone. That day, he came home, and my thoughts went out to greet him, when I encountered a barrier that was difficult to pierce. This is when I was confronted by the M.S. that had invaded his mind. It affected me in a horrible way, and I could hardly move. My father, or whatever that being was that was in my father's body, gathered me up in his arms and kissed me. Then he sat down, placing me on his lap. All the while I was reading his mind. His thoughts were all about the imminent destruction of our world, for the following day he planned to explode the subterranean atom bomb stores to let our continent go up into the air.

"Who would have believed my story? I was just a little six year old girl. I acted automatically. The gun he used to carry in his pocket flew into my hand by way of telekinesis. And then . . . well, then that's how it happened."

Ellert remained silent. He let compassionate thoughts flow gently around the little girl. She lifted up her head, looking to the sky, where she presumed Ellert's spirit to be.

"And now, Ernst, go back to Rhodan and report what you have found out about me. There is one thing I can tell you—the M.S. invasion will fail! We will defeat them. But you, Ernst . . ."

Her thoughts grew dim, he could no longer perceive them.

"Go on—what is the matter with me, Betty?"

"I am sorry. I can't tell you."

"Why not?"

"I am not allowed to, Ernst. Please, don't insist any further. You are the pivot around which the whole future history of mankind revolves. You are the turning point of human history. Your fate is closely linked with that of the galactic empire of a far distant future. If you had any idea of what lies in store you might try to avoid it. That must not happen. Go along the path that your fate has chosen for you, so that Perry Rhodan can reach his goal. You and I will never see each other again."

"And in five years . . . now? What is going to be then? Where will I be?"

"In another five years? You will look upon this time as the dawn of mankind. You will look upon it from some lofty viewpoint that surpasses all human imagination. And now, will you please leave me alone."

Ellert felt that Betty Toufry was erecting a shell around her mind, a shell he was unable to pierce. A few more seconds of indecision and then he returned to the present time.

He knew exactly what he had to do.

CHAPTER FOUR

"You are convinced that the invaders' base here on Earth is somewhere in Tibet?" asked Reginald Bell.

Rhodan nodded. Khrest was sitting next to him. Rhodan held a sheaf of papers in his hand, the latest reports from the G.C.C., telling about the new factories and industrial installations that Adams was having built in all parts of the globe. He had already started the construction of the terrestrial space fleet. The borders between the world's nations seemed to have come down finally, at least in this respect.

"I know for sure, Reg. The M.S. intend to have Li proceed to their base. What their plans are once he gets there we unfortunately do not know, though. The M.S. changed their minds once they became aware of Ellert's mind probing inside the brain of Dr. Lehmann, who in turn had been taken over by one of the M.S. They did not abandon Li's body and select a new target. Li traveled to Nevada Spaceport and there met Dr. Lehmann. I am sure that the two have orders to deal a serious blow to our space exploration program there."

"I have no idea how to prevent the two from carrying out their orders," remarked Khrest. He still seemed to doubt that anyone could ever manage to resist the M.S. His own decadent race had become too tired to fight effectively against the invaders. "They have conquered whole star systems and subjugated entire races, and nobody could prevent it.

"We most certainly will!" said Rhodan, hard and determined. "We have the means to do it, too. The disastrous atom bomb had something in its favor, despite the havoc it wreaked on part of mankind. Atomic radiation resulted in accelerating the development of the human race by a thousand times. Whatever man would have developed into within ten thousand years, he has already become today, at least partially so. Our mutant corps is nothing but the precursor of the future human norm. And this did not happen any too soon, for without the assistance of our mutants we would be the helpless victims at the mercy of a merciless foe."

Khrest looked straight at Rhodan. There was a fire burning in the golden hued eyes below his mighty brow—the same fire that Rhodan had once before perceived in them when they were discussing Earth's future fate linked with that of the Arkonide empire. Khrest's gaze was filled with admiration, joy, and trust, mixed with some worry. All this against a background of the unlimited knowledge of an age old race that had witnessed the rise and fall of many solar systems.

"I have lately been preoccupied with the question whether fate or accident rules the universe," he replied. "I am almost inclined to lean toward fate playing the decisive role. How powerful and inconceivable must be the might of the one who has to weigh the decisions. . . ."

"As far as our little world here is concerned, we are the ones to decide," interjected Bell in his usual prosaic manner. Quickly he changed the subject to what was now nearest to their hearts. "What will happen in Nevada?"

Rhodan smiled enigmatically. "We will set a trap for them. In case they get caught in it, which seems most likely the way things stand at the present time, we should know shortly if we will win or lose our battle against the invading enemy. It all depends on whether Ellert's theory works out in practice."

"Do you really believe his theory that our teleporters can pursue the disembodied minds of the Mind Snatchers when they leave their victim's bodies in a kind of a panic?"

"Yes, I do believe this to be feasible, Khrest," confirmed Rhodan. "This will be our only chance to discover their hiding place. Once we are that far, the rest should not be too difficult. We might even be lucky and catch one of the M.S. in their natural form. Talking about this, I am reminded of a splendid suggestion that Ellert made to me. But all this depends on the outcome of the experiment in Nevada."

"How about letting us in on the big secret!" urged Bell. "What are you planning to do there?"

"That won't take long to explain. You, too, should listen carefully, Khrest, I plan the following. . . ."

The new element had all the necessary prerequisites to become the future ideal propellant for space travel. It took up very little space in its solid form, which was one of its greatest advantages. Furthermore, it was absolutely harmless as long as it was not exposed to some harmless type of radiation, which could be produced at any time with the help of simple instruments. If that radiation process took place, then an atomic structural change was induced, which in turn depended on the intensity of the radiation. This radiation then was a catalyst; without it the new element remained nothing but a useless piece of metal.

The experiments had not yet been concluded. Dr. Lehmann had succeeded in creating this new element. It was so cheap to produce that a trip to Mars would cost no more than a bus ride around town. Of course, this cost was negligible once the spaceship had been built. With the application of the radiation it was possible to release as much energy as was needed at that point. This new propellant would be ideal for faster than light flight.

Of course, this was still only theory. But Dr. Lehmann was so obsessed by this idea that no one could deter him from carrying out the final experiments. One of the final steps was supposed to take place today.

As the official representative of Allan D. Mercant, Li had access to all the installations of the research area. Lehmann would have been the last to object to his presence, since he knew Li to be really an M.S. like himself. The invaders intended to overexpose the new element to the catalytic radiation. This would result in an irreversible chain reaction, which would lead to the total destruction of the research center. Afterward, the two M.S. would leave the now useless bodies of their unwilling hosts and look for new victims. This was the point where some changes would occur.

Ellert had claimed that only a panicky M.S. would flee in such a manner that could be pursued. Great hurry would preclude the necessary preparation for the flight. Ellert had argued that this would not leave them sufficient time to build up a protective mental screen that would blur the trail leading into another dimension. Although this sounded rather confusing, it was nevertheless convincing.

This was why the catastrophe planned by Li and Lehmann had to be brought about as quick as lightning and then had to be stopped just in time, after the two M.S.

had abandoned their two host bodies in a hurry. They would be forced to such haste unless they chose to die together with their victims' bodies.

Lehmann and Li entered the room that housed the atomic reactor. They were in the company of John Marshall. Nothing seemed to arouse Lehmann's suspicion. The lab assistants greeted him and then turned to their work again. He obviously recognized them as being regularly employed in the lab. He hardly noticed, though, two or three new employees; least of all the new electrician, Ellert, who was busy with some levers located close to the huge switch gear box. Anne Sloane, who was scheduled to play the most important part in the coming catastrophe, was stationed inconspicuously somewhere in the background of the maze of instruments and installations.

A dull thud marked the closing of the heavy lead door, the only access to the reactor center. Lehmann knew that a push from the inside would open it again. As soon as the chain reaction started there would be enough time left to get out of that lab and reach the safety of their own rooms, from where they would then leave to return to their own insect bodies.

Lehmann, together with Li and Marshall, stepped over to the lead chamber. He pointed to a brick shaped metal bar that gleamed suspiciously behind the pane of quartz.

"This is the new element, gentlemen. If we send an electric current through these points over there a radiation process is started that passes through the element, thus bringing about structural changes. So far we have not yet succeeded in making full use of the energy set free. The energy is changed into heat, which registers over there on that temperature gauge. The inside walls of the lead chamber are highly heat resistant. The whole process must be increased only very gradually to avoid a sudden blowout. Well, you two laymen won't be able to appreciate the full extent of the progress that is hidden in this apparently insignificant looking piece of metal in there. Its energy would be sufficient to propel a spaceship halfway through the universe at the speed of light."

Lehmann walked over to the switchboard. For a moment he contemplated Ellert, who was dressed in a white lab coat. Ellert acted as if he had known the professor for a long time, realizing, though, that such a famous man could not be bothered to remember every little employee working in the lab. Similar thoughts were racing through the M.S. mind that was dwelling in Lehmann's brain.

"Is everything okay?" asked the scientist.

"In perfect working order, Professor," confirmed Ellert, whose whole knowledge of the complicated machinery was limited to the manipulation of one single lever. This was the lever that regulated the switching on and off of the electric current that in turn determined the intensity of the radiation.

"Fine, switch to the minimum."

The lever flipped into the first notch. There were twenty of these notches. No one in his right mind would ever dare pull the lever over to the last notch, not even Lehmann, for this would cause the change to occur so rapidly that in all probability the whole lead chamber would melt immediately.

No change could be observed behind the quartz pane, but the temperature gauge began to rise.

Lehmann expressed satisfaction. "Heat! The temperature is rising. This position on the first notch would be enough to supply a whole continent with enough energy for hundreds of years. It's incredible, isn't it?"

Li was standing next to Lehmann. He was silent. There was, after all, no need for words between him and his fellow M.S. in the form of Lehmann. They communicated telepathically. It was not difficult for Marshall to probe cautiously these quick thoughts that rushed back and forth between the two aliens' minds. John had to be very careful not to make them suspicious of him. His scientific knowledge was too limited to appreciate the full extent of Lehmann's scientific achievement, but he did understand Li's question, "What is the critical point?"

"When the lever goes up to the seventh notch," replied Lehmann via telepathy. But the words he spoke out loud to Ellert were, "Advance the lever another notch!"

Ellert comprehended the devilish plan the M.S. had hatched out. Lehmann would ask him gradually to increase the amount of energy until the seventh notch was reached, at which point the process would become irreversible and a chain reaction would set in. But all this would proceed at a very slow rate. Thus the two M.S. could leave the reactor room in all leisure, return to their rooms, and proceed to transfer their minds back to their own bodies, while in the meantime, here inside the reactor, the unleashed forces would begin their disastrous work.

Anne Sloane realized that the time had come for her to act. Under no circumstances must Ellert be disturbed now. Like John Marshall, he must be able to concentrate fully on the two M.S. in order to follow them on their headlong flight. Ellert would leave his own body, yet remain in the present time. John would recognize the exact instant when the M.S. decided to flee. He would signal to the man who so far had kept inconspicuously in a faraway corner behind one of the huge generators. Tako Kakuta, the teleporter, would dematerialize his body and follow the M.S., the same as Ellert.

Nothing could go wrong now, unless they had overlooked something. This did not seem likely, thought Ellert, who had stepped back from the switchboard.

Lehmann observed the rising temperature gauge. A fanatic gleam was in his eye. He no longer tried to keep up the pretense. Li, on the other hand, remained calm.

"Move the lever up to seven!" commanded Lehmann unexpectedly.

The moment had come!

Anne Sloane approached. Her eyes were fixed on the lever on Ellert's instrument panel. The lever began to move slowly, going beyond the seventh notch, advancing further and further. At the same time the total reserve current from the generators passed through the reactor, transformed into radiation that penetrated the metal block of the new element. Then it was caught again, ready to start the whole process over again. Anne knew that this could go on for twenty seconds before serious damage could result. For then a chain reaction would set in that could not be stopped. No one would be able to escape the inferno that would break loose inside the reactor room, if the only door could not be opened.

She turned around and directed her glance toward the heavy lead door. The invisible energies of her mind penetrated the metal and bolted the exit from the outside. Now the door could no longer be pushed open from the inside.

They were all prisoners in a burning hell that was about to turn everything into incandescent gas.

Twenty seconds were left, not an instant more.

Professor Lehmann spun around. For a moment he lost his composure when he saw the lever approach the maximum point. The lever seemed to be moved by some invisible hand. Lehmann was so startled by this sight that he let precious seconds elapse before he could search his memory banks for the necessary information for such an emergency. Now he knew! It would take twenty seconds before the catastrophe set in. But before he managed to reach the lever and push it back into a safe position, the electric circuit blew out under the overload. Sparks were flying and lightning flashes jumped across the burst fuses. Lehmann shrank back when he saw the lever melt and assume a distorted shape due to the tremendous heat. The stench of burned rubber and melting metal filled his nostrils. There was a smell of ozone in the air.

Li stood rooted to the spot. Hastily he tried to confer with Lehmann, who did not pay any attention to him. He was still preoccupied trying to solve the riddle of the mysteriously moving lever. He could not arrive at an explanation. Then it dawned on him that only immediate flight could save him. He was so terrified that he forgot the five seconds that still remained, which would have given him all the time he needed for an orderly retreat.

The heavy lead door would not budge. Fifteen seconds had passed. The catastrophe was imminent.

Sixteen seconds. Now it was too late to open the way into another dimension. The two M.S. understood that no way out existed but to abandon the human bodies on the spot unless they wished to perish together with them. Without the necessary preparation they withdrew and forced their way into a world that is exclusively reserved for disembodied intellects. They left behind the lifeless, rigid bodies of the two men who were awaiting the return of their original spirits. That would happen only at the twenty-first second . . . and that would be too late!

John Marshall gave the arranged signal to Tako Kakuta, waiting in the background. The Japanese dematerialized and disappeared. He connected himself to the matterless stream of the fleeing M.S. and let himself be carried toward an unknown destination. The pursuit was much simpler than he had imagined.

Seventeen seconds.

Anne Sloane concentrated on the white hot lever and tried to apply all her reserves to push it back to point zero. But she failed. A few drops of the molten metal had dripped down and congealed. Her strength was not enough to overcome this obstacle. She could not understand why. She knew that she was capable of lifting weights of several tons by the sheer power of her mind. But now she had to capitulate before that ridiculous lever. The strain had been too much for her. She was now completely exhausted.

Eighteen seconds.

"Ellert . . . the lever! I can't move it!"

Nineteen seconds. One more second to eternity!

Ellert did not hesitate. He leaped over to the panel and pushed with all his force against the deformed lever. A hissing sound could be heard; then with a sudden jolt the powerful pressure wrenched loose the molten metal drops that had glued the lever in the twentieth notch. Smoothly the lever slid back to point zero. At the same time the current found a more direct path than the wide leap across the interrupted wires. A bluish white flash jumped from the machine and disappeared in Ellert's body.

The teletemporarian collapsed. His burned arm gave off a terrible stench.

But the catastrophe had been averted.

Before the twentieth second had come, the lever rested on zero.

In the twenty-first second, Lehmann and Li began to stir. Life returned to their bodies. At first they looked in consternation at everything around them, especially Li, who had never before in all his life been inside such a scientific research laboratory. He recognized John Marshall and Anne Sloane. Then he saw the lifeless form of Ellert sprawled on the floor near him. He had no idea what was going on in this room.

It was a different story with the professor. Although he could not figure out how he had come so suddenly from his chess board to this switchboard, he naturally recognized the familiar surroundings of his usual place of work.

He remembered the experiment he had been so long preparing. And finally he noticed Marshall.

"What has happened?" he asked quietly. "I can't remember . . ."

"Later, Professor," interrupted John. "A lot has happened, and you will understand everything. But right now there are more urgent matters. Is there still any danger here, Lehmann? The metal bar inside the lead chamber was exposed to the most intense radiation for nineteen seconds. Will that cause a chain reaction?"

Lehmann stared at Marshall.

"Nineteen seconds? On notch twenty? Who ordered that?"

"Never mind that, just answer my question—*now*, Professor!"

Lehmann shook his head. "The limit of stabilization lies at about twenty seconds."

"Okay. Then we have time to look after Ellert. Miss Sloane, get a doctor, quick!"

Dr. Fleeps seemed to have a sixth sense, for hardly had Anne pushed back the outside bolt on the heavy lead door, using again her telekinetic powers, than the specialist for space medicine stormed into the reactor room.

"I was told that our instruments recorded unusual fluctuations in the electric current here. . . ."

"One of our men was careless and was electrocuted," explained John Marshall.

Ellert had remained motionless on the floor. He was stretched out, a limp, lifeless corpse. Now it was possible to see that his arm had been totally burned up to his elbow. Nothing but a stump remained.

Still, this injury could not be fatal, unless the electric shock . . .

Dr. Fleeps bent over Ellert and began to examine him. In the meantime John Marshall explained everything that had occurred to the perplexed professor. Li listened with amazement. This was beyond all plausibility, as far as he was concerned.

Anne waited next to Dr. Fleeps. She felt responsible for what had happened to Ellert. If she hadn't failed in her efforts, all would have been different. She was at a loss why her telekinetic energy had not been sufficient to move the lever. Had the excitement proved to be too much of a distraction for her?

Dr. Fleeps straightened out. "That's odd," he mumbled. "That man is alive."

John Marshall turned around slowly.

Anne Sloane asked, "He is alive? Thank heavens! What should there be so odd about that?"

"Ten thousand volts!" he marveled. He gazed at the motionless body of Ellert. "Strange that he could survive that."

Dr. Fleeps shook his head. "You did not quite understand me. He is alive, but only from a biological point of view. But at the same time he is also a dead man, biologically."

All stared at the doctor. No one spoke. The temperature gauge of the lead chamber had slowly returned to normal.

"How can a human being be alive and dead at the same time?" asked Professor Lehmann, whose scientific curiosity had been aroused. "That would be a paradox."

"You are right according to the laws of logic," admitted the physician. It was plainly to be seen how confused he was and how he tried in vain to hide it. "But where does logic come into all these strange phenomena we have been witnessing lately? Can these alien invaders be reconciled with our concepts of logic and reality? Haven't these strange creatures come to us from a universe where our scientific laws have no application? I am therefore not at all surprised to see in this man a living dead person."

"What makes you think so?"

Dr. Fleeps pointed to the floor where Ellert was lying without movement. "He is no longer breathing; no pulse, no heartbeat, no circulation. How long since this accident happened?"

John looked at his watch. "About ten minutes ago."

"A certain drop in body temperature should already have taken place. But I can't detect a trace of it. I wouldn't be surprised if his temperature remains at around ninety-seven degrees Fahrenheit."

"But how can that be?"

"Sorry. I can't explain this myself. I can just register a fact, that's all. Ellert is neither dead nor alive. It is as if his soul had left his body."

John Marshall looked at Anne. There was no one here

besides themselves and Li who knew of Ellert's special abilities. Perhaps the teletemporarian had executed a leap through time in order to save his life. Who could know the truth? Only then when he came back again . . .

"I think Perry Rhodan should be the judge of all this. Let him make any decisions that need to be done," interjected Anne Sloane. "I will inform him at once of what has occurred here."

Professor Lehmann took his eyes off Ellert. "And what happened—what happened to the M.S. that have fled from our bodies?"

"We might find out soon," answered John Marshall, and left the reactor room in the company of Li and Anne Sloane. Only Dr. Fleeps and a very perplexed Professor Lehmann stayed behind.

CHAPTER FIVE

Tako Kakuta felt himself swept up by a giant whirlpool that dragged him down with irresistible force.

For the first time he became consciously aware of the current in which he was traveling. Normally this state lasted but a fraction of a second, during which his dematerialized body was transported from one place to another. He neither saw nor heard anything, but he could feel with every particle of his body.

Maybe he was traveling through darkness that did not permit him to see. But before he had time to figure out this strange phenomenon, he had materialized again.

As far as he could guess, just five seconds had elapsed.

It was still dark around him, but now his body had taken on shape again. Gradually the darkness began to lift, and he saw a faint glow coming from the surrounding walls. He had the impression of being in a big hall. It was quite cool.

Something on the floor near his feet began to stir. Now his eyes had become adjusted to the dim light and he recognized the elongated forms that rested next to each other on the hard, rocky ground.

It took several more seconds before the realization dawned on him of what these shapes were. The sudden insight made him wince in fear. There they were stretched out in long rows, the bodies of the Mind Snatchers, immobilized in a cataleptic state, serving as a prison for the human spirits while the invaders' minds had taken over their human frames. Two of the rigid shapes started to move. These must be the ones that belonged to the two M.S. that shortly before had dwelt in Professor Lehmann's and Li's bodies.

Tako knew he could not waste another second. He dematerialized again and stood almost immediately on a wide, stony plain. In the distance loomed the white peaks of the Himalaya Mountains. He estimated the direction and distance of his jump. The hall where the M.S. bodies were lying was three miles to the south. He could make out a mountain there, not too high but rather massive.

That hall he had been in was a natural cave. Of course; that was to be expected!

Tako Kakuta manipulated the bracelet around his left wrist. Seconds later he could hear Perry Rhodan's voice. "We guessed correctly, Tako. Tibet! Where exactly are you? I am six miles above the Himalayas."

"I don't know for sure. Couldn't you get a fix on me?"

"Just a moment. Reg is at the direction finder. It will take a couple of seconds for us to locate you. Have you found the M.S. base?"

"Everything went in perfect order, according to plan, the way Ellert predicted. By the way, why didn't Ellert accompany me?"

Brief silence. Then Rhodan said, "An unfortunate incident occurred we had not foreseen. Ellert was electrocuted. His body is on its way to the Gobi Desert base."

Tako was unable to reply. He just waited until finally Rhodan continued. "Who knows, something else might have happened to him, and he isn't dead after all. We aren't sure yet . . . Here we are, Reg has located you. We are one hundred twenty miles to the east from where you are. We'll join you shortly."

Tako walked over to a large rock and sat down. The sun was setting in the west, and soon darkness would fall. He did not know Rhodan's plans, but warding off the invasion had become a worldwide enterprise where one factor encroached upon the other until no one knew any longer what his role was in the overall picture. Only one man had the total overview of the strategy. That man was Perry Rhodan.

Silently the huge space sphere landed on the plateau. The antigrav beam seized Tako and lifted him up before he had a chance to teleport himself into the interior of the ship. Good naturedly, he tolerated Bell's transporting him in such a conservative method into the center where Rhodan was already waiting for him.

"Thanks to your efforts, Tako, we have found the enemy's base here on Earth. Now it is up to us to put him out of action completely. Thora has promised to assist us in that unconditionally. She is deathly afraid of the Mind Snatchers, which I fully understand. Khrest is with her at the battle station. I have taken over the command for navigation and general coordination of all efforts. Where is the cave, Tako?"

The Japanese pointed to the screen. "Over there, that low mountain. Inside, about sixty feet below the surface."

"A natural cave in the Himalayas," said Rhodan with a bitter smile. "That's like them, just what I thought they would do."

The *Good Hope* lifted off vertically without any apparent effort and slid over to the hill Tako had pointed out. The spacecraft hovered above it while Perry Rhodan gave some orders to Thora. Then he turned to Tako and Bell, who had remained standing just inside the door.

"The attack will take place in thirty seconds. Thora is going to evaporate that part of the mountain directly above the cave. Let's hope that we can find an entrance to the cave; otherwise, we risk burning the bodies of the M.S. I am very interested in catching some of them alive."

Tako seemed skeptical. "Is that advisable? Wouldn't they take over our own bodies at once?"

"Don't worry," Rhodan reassured him. "I shall apply the psychoradiator."

The psychoradiator was one of the harmless weapons of the Arkonides. Whoever used it was capable of imposing his own will on the target personality. Even posthypnotic commands could be given, and they had to be obeyed unconditionally. Rhodan hoped that the psychoradiator would have the usual effect even if applied to the insect type aliens.

Suddenly a strong wind sprang up over the flat mountain peak. Cold air masses rushed in from all sides into the heated airspace above it. The whole mountain top began to evaporate. The rocks turned into invisible gases that rose up. So tremendous was the effect of the energy rays that the transition of matter from solid to gaseous state followed almost immediately without first passing through the liquid phase.

At a depth of sixty feet a dark opening became visible.

"The entrance!" shouted Rhodan, and stopped the attack. The space sphere descended and touched the ground. Seconds later the airlocks opened and Perry, Reg, Khrest, and Thora rushed out into the open. Tako was already waiting for them outside. He had preferred to use the much more convenient teleportation.

"I've already been inside again," he announced. "The opening here leads into the cave, just a few feet from here. Hurry! Two of the nasty creatures are moving. They look horrid!"

Perry Rhodan hurried ahead of the others, the silvery rod of the psychoradiator glistening in his hand. He had to bend over on entering the low passageway leading to the cave. The others followed at a slower pace, especially Reg, who had a lot of trouble avoiding constant collision of his broad shoulders with the rocky walls of the narrow path. Khrest and Thora kept in the background.

Unexpectedly the narrow passage widened into a wide hall. Perry's eyes had to accommodate to the darkness. The walls sent out a slight phosphoresence. A draft came from a corner; there must be another exit to the cave.

Reg kept close behind Rhodan. The illuminating rod in his hand lit up, throwing a bright light across the whole extent of the underground cave. The first thing they noticed was the long row of lifeless bodies resting on the ground. They were slightly taller than human beings but looked quite different. They closely resembled insects.

A cry of horror rent the stillness. Reg had screamed involuntarily. His hand that held the light trembled.

Even Rhodan had trouble overcoming his feelings of shock and fright. Although he had been mentally prepared to face the Mind Snatchers in person, their appearance exceeded his worst expectations.

Six feet away stood the two extraterrestrial monsters

who had come to Earth to subjugate the human race. No, even worse than that! For they would not hesitate to destroy the whole planet. They simply did not tolerate any other races; that was all. An unbridled drive to destroy was at the root of all their actions.

The two monsters resembled gigantically distorted wasps but differed from these insects in many respects. They did have the typical wasp waist, as well as six limbs. Two of these limbs served as legs on which they were standing upright. Their multifaceted insect eyes glistened maliciously. Two shiny antennae played excitedly above their pointed heads. Their thoraxes looked hard and sturdy.

Perry Rhodan wasted no time. He directed the beam of his psychoradiator against the two monsters and ordered them to make an about-face. Although he had counted on this maneuver's success, he could not help feeling relieved when the two M.S. carried out his instructions without the slightest sign of resistance. Therefore, he concluded, their brain structure had to resemble that of man. This similarity would in the final analysis become the decisive factor that would permit the human race to win out over their enemies, the Mind Snatchers.

"Walk up to the surface and do whatever you are told by Tako Kakuta!" Rhodan continued. Then he added to the Japanese, "Wait up there with them until I can join you."

As Tako led his two charges past Bell, the hefty engineer, not normally given to fear, began to shudder and tremble involuntarily. Reg felt as if Death in person had brushed against him.

"We have never come as close as that to them," remarked Khrest in a feeble attempt to justify his own race's lack of success in dealing with the menace of the M.S. "We never believed it would be possible to make use of the psychoradiator in our fight against them."

"I was absolutely convinced that the psychoradiator would be effective against the M.S., although I had no concrete basis for my belief," said Rhodan, at the same time pointing out one of the important differences between the mentality of his own race and that of the Arkonide scientist. Being able to convert a mere belief into a scientific fact demanded a type of energy that the Arkonides had lost as their race had grown older and more decadent.

Thora's face plainly showed her feelings of deep repulsion as she stared at the immobile row of lifeless bodies. The energy gun in her hand was poised as if ready for action.

"No, Thora, not yet. Hold it!" he warned her. "There is too much at stake here. If we should destroy these twenty-two insect bodies here, we would condemn twenty-two dematerialized human personalities to be in limbo forever. For they cannot return to their own human frames unless they have been vacated by the M.S. usurpers, which is of course out of the question, once the M.S. have lost their own bodies. We can destroy these insect bodies only after their minds have taken up abode in them again. Then, naturally, we must act quickly."

"Twenty-two human beings?" replied Thora with deliberate slowness. "Aren't they worth a victory over our common enemy?"

"I would not hesitate to sacrifice them, if necessary," Rhodan admitted in a somber voice. "But that isn't the point. At all costs, we must avoid twenty-two M.S. in disguise wreaking havoc here on Earth. Do you understand what I mean? Someone will have to remain here in this cave to watch for the moment the M.S. minds return. As soon as the bodies start moving they must be destroyed."

A sudden insight seemed to come over Thora. The disgust in her eyes disappeared and in its place came something new. Perry Rhodan had observed the same change in her once before. Now her eyes expressed appreciation and even respect.

Respect . . . for whom? wondered Rhodan. For himself or perhaps for mankind? That would mean tremendous progress, worth far more than a battle victory against the invaders. But perhaps his eyes were deceived by the dim light inside the underground cave. Nevertheless, couldn't there have occurred a change in Thora's attitude toward Earthlings? Learning to recognize one's own shortcomings is usually achieved only by the intelligent. And there was certainly no lack of intelligence in the brilliant Thora!

"Who is going to stay behind?" she asked.

Rhodan smiled. "I guess Reg would be the ideal man for that job—"

Before Rhodan could finish his sentence he was interrupted by a scream. A very frightened Reg was now pointing to one of the reclining shapes on the ground before them. The monstrous creature began to stir and to sit up halfway, staring with vacant eyes into the bright light of Bell's lamp.

Perry Rhodan lightly touched Thora's arm. "If you feel like it, you can kill the thing. Just remember that these Mind Snatchers are the mortal foes of your nation. Unless we check their advance they will swarm over the Arkonide empire like a horde of locusts, devouring and annihilating everything in their path. They will bring about the end of the Arkonide rule in the universe. Don't be frightened of killing this beast. Just a few moments ago that was all you could think about."

The beautiful alien female raised her weapon, still hesitating, and aimed at the giant wasp whose black eyes still gazed into the blinding circle of light. The mere sight of the insect filled Thora with such fear and trepidation that she quickly overcame her misgivings of killing another living being while face to face with it.

She pulled the trigger. A violet ray shot out and hit the insect's abdomen. The violent pain jerked the M.S. out of his initial lethargic state. But it was too late; it could no longer react. It could not even send a message of warning to the oval shaped spaceship that was cruising beyond the Earth's atmosphere.

A burning hole showed on the insect's body and a line of fire traveled up to its thorax. The giant wasp collapsed.

Thora lowered her weapon. "It was horrible!" she exclaimed, handing the gun to Rhodan. "I could never do that again."

"But it will have to be done another twenty-one times," replied Rhodan, taking the ray gun and passing it to his friend Reg, who was obviously reluctant to accept it. "Reg, you know what to do, don't you?"

"I won't stay here all alone," protested Bell.

"Tako can keep you company," suggested Rhodan.

"He won't be any help," grumbled Reg. "As soon as things get too hot, he'll just take off with one of his famous jumps and leave me here to face the mess." But then Bell accepted the ray gun from Rhodan's hands and looked grimly along the line of the reposing insect bodies.

"Our task is not yet completed," said Rhodan before he turned to leave. "There are still another twenty-one invaders busy out there in the disguise of influential men in high posts. Their aim is to bring chaos and destruction to our world. We must track them down and then force them to flee back into their own bodies here. Fortunately we know who they are. So this won't present too much of a problem for us. I imagine, Reg, that we will pick you up tonight or sometime tomorrow morning. In the meantime I have to inform Mercant and our mutant corps and tell them how to proceed. Have fun here, Reg. Tako will help you while the time away!"

Bell was so stunned at the prospect before him that he did not immediately vent his feelings. By the time he managed to utter a strong, one syllable comment, his friend had long since disappeared.

The same instant that Ellert touched the ill fated lever of the electro panel a strange event took place. The strangest part was that he experienced everything while fully conscious and never lost his awareness for a single moment.

Unbearable pain raced through his body, then faded quickly. The space around him fell away into a bottomless abyss that knew neither beginning nor end. Colorful reflections whirled about him, sometimes enveloping him from close by, then receding again into the distance. Undefinable sounds, abstract and devoid of harmony, thronged into his ears, or whatever served him now as auditory receptacles. These impressions came and went again in a rhythmical succession, as if he had entered the interior of a pulsating universe.

There was nothing above him; there was nothing below him. He was floating in the void. At one time a sun with rotating planets whizzed by somewhere in the distance, far, far away. Galaxies were slowly rotating like spinning tops, and then they too disappeared somewhere deep into space. Eternity seemed to shrink into nothing.

With a speed that was beyond comprehension, Ellert was racing through the stream of time, over which he had lost any control. He was hurled into an infinity devoid of any matter. The present time remained behind the way Earth would recede from a radar beam rushing out into space.

Nothing could impede his plunge into the future.

And then, all of a sudden, he felt ground under his feet again. So sudden was this materialization, so unexpected, that he collapsed and lost consciousness. How long he had been lying there, he could never have told later on. But on awakening he became aware of his body. Had he returned to the present time, or had he overtaken his own body some time in the future? He dismissed the question the same instant he had posed it.

Millions of years must have elapsed, for he had witnessed the growth and death of entire universe islands. He could never live that long.

But he did possess a body!

He felt the silky fur and grew frightened. When finally he managed to open his eyes, his wildest fears were confirmed. His mind, which had been flung into a far distant future, had found a new abode, but it was not the body of a human being that sheltered him now.

The monster was four-legged and had only a very limited intelligence, which left ample space for Ellert's mind inside the huge skull. A soft fur covered the monster's body. Could this be a bear? Ellert wondered. But he soon realized his mistake. For inside him was suddenly a voice. . . .

"I am Gorx," said the toneless voice. "Who are you?"

Ellert was startled, but he managed to think back. "I am Ellert. Why aren't you surprised . . . ?"

"Why should I be surprised that you came? We often get visitors from the universe."

"Where am I?"

"Our world is called Gorx," came the information.

"And what do you call your sun?"

"Gorx."

Ellert was puzzled. He could not understand. "Why is everything here called Gorx?"

"Everything is called Gorx because everything *is* Gorx."

The explanation seemed sheer insanity to Ellert. How could he ever learn where fate had brought him? Or was this what the planet Earth would be like millions of years in the future? He dismissed this question too before he even tried it. He knew that the shock of his physical death had flung him not only through time but also through space.

Ellert made a concerted effort and left his host's body.

Way down below him he saw a heavy, furry creature crawl clumsily over the rocky ground. He could discern dark entrances to caves over there at the vertical rock walls.

Here he would not be able to find any answers to his questions. Not here!

Once again the world disappeared from underneath him and gave way to infinity.

Ellert whirled anew through the time stream, but this time in the opposite direction—he traveled back in time. When he could once again stop in his fall, he was floating again in the void.

How could he ever find his way back to the present time? There was no point where he could find his bearings and get a fix on time. He was like a tiny drop of water in an ocean, a drop that was supposed to touch land at a certain spot of one of the six continents, at a certain predetermined point in time that was measured by seconds.

The inevitable realization dawned on Ellert—he could never return to his own time and space. He had become the prisoner of an eternity whose master he had believed himself to be.

No longer did the qustion matter *where* he was. He was confronted by the more horrible uncertainty of *when* he was. . . .

There was no answer to that question. Unless eternity itself could supply the solution.

And thus Ellert, the prisoner of eternity, began his quest for the present time, a search that would last for millions of years. . . .

CHAPTER SIX

The worker robots had completed their task. The tunnel penetrated the stony ground of the Gobi Desert to a depth of one hundred fifty feet. Steel hard enameled walls would ensure protection against the ravages of erosion for all time. Neither could any ground water seep through these walls into the shaft. At the bottom of the tunnel, Rhodan had the robots construct a rectangular room that contained oxygen supplies, all kinds of information, instructions, and energy reservoirs. An automic installation would set everything in motion the moment it was needed.

In the middle of the twelve by twelve foot chamber stood a couch. Attached to it was a very complicated alarm system, which would be activated the very instant the human being inside the room took his first breath.

This human being was Ernst Ellert.

They had placed him under the electronic instruments. Metal clasps enclosed his left wrist and both ankles. A helmet had been put on his head. Close to his mouth they had suspended a mirror connected to selenium cells. The faintest exhalation would be sufficient to set the whole installation in motion.

This mausoleum had been constructed by Rhodan for Ellert. The building was unlike anything ever built for any mortal. But Rhodan intuitively knew that Ellert was no mere mortal. Rhodan carried the deep conviction that someday he would meet up again with the teletemporarian.

But it might also be possible that Ellert would find his way back by himself. Then he should be able to find his own body in a perfect state, unravaged by the damages that time normally would inflict on the human body. The three physicians—Dr. Fleeps, Dr. Manoli, and Dr. Haggard —were of the same opinion: Ellert's body would never decompose, despite the fact that it had stopped all metabolic functions. Yet his body temperature never fell below ninety-seven degrees Fahrenheit.

Rhodan glanced for the last time at the quietly reposing Ellert; then he gave the order to seal the burial chamber. Ten minutes later liquid concrete was poured into the shaft, which soon was filled with a solid core. Nothing in the world would ever disturb the rest of this body—nothing except the harmless looking apparatus under the ceiling of the burial chamber, waiting there to be put into action. If ever Ellert should awaken inside the tomb he would be able to set himself free within half an hour. But what would he find? A world revolving close to a red sun into which it threatened to fall at any moment? Or a planet that had been swept clean of any life by an invasion from space?

There might never be an answer to these questions. Who could predict?

Lost in deep thought, Rhodan watched as the robots placed a pyramid shaped cone above the spot that led down into the burial chamber. In the distance the mighty sphere of the *Good Hope* shimmered in the bright desert sun. . . .

All throughout his return flight to Gobi City, as Reginald Bell had privately named the Third Power's Gobi Desert base, his mood was dark and depressed. He had taken twenty-one lives during the past twenty-four hours. As he kept reassuring himself, these had not been human lives, but still he had deprived some beings of their life. Had he been justified to kill?

He had had ample time to discuss this question with Tako, but they had not arrived at a satisfactory solution. No doubt, they had acted in self-defense. For unless they had immediately destroyed the M.S. upon their reentry into their own insect bodies, the creatures would have given the alarm to their oval shaped command ship circling far above the Earth. Or else they might have taken possession of both his and Tako's brains.

No, Rhodan was right. Leniency was out of place here; it was far too dangerous. The invaders had chosen to take a calculated risk when they attacked Earth. They had lost and must therefore accept punishment. This still need not mean that they would give up the fight.

The oval shaped spaceship had been a worry to Reginald Bell. So far it had not been possible to pinpoint its location. Either the distance from Earth was too great or the enemy craft had hidden out somewhere. But where?

This was the question Bell asked of his friend Perry Rhodan after rejoining the desert base.

Rhodan pondered awhile before he replied, "There seem to be no more Mind Snatchers here on Earth, as far as we know. Their spacecraft might be hiding out, and I have an inkling where that might be. I placed the two prisoners into a hypnotrance. Manoli and Haggard examined them. According to their report they discovered astonishing anatomical differences between theirs and the human body. The M.S. do not possess a language the way we do. They are telepaths. A great part of their brain consists of a complicated organic transmitter and receiver structure. We fear that they are capable of communicating over distances that amount to light-years."

"Have you been able to talk to them—I mean, to establish some telepathic rapport?"

"Yes, thanks to Marshall I have been able to communicate with them."

"Well, and what did you find out?"

"Unfortunately not too much. They are very stubborn, and I had to apply the hypnoradiator to make them 'talk,' if you'll pardon this human expression. Still, they could not divulge any more than they themselves knew. They did want to destroy our planet. Yes, you heard me right—destroy it completely. They had no political or economical interest in our world. They were not driven by any imperialistic motives to take over our Earth. They simply came to annihilate us, for they cannot tolerate anyone besides themselves. Therefore, we need not have any qualms if we fight back just as mercilessly. It is a question of survival—them or us!"

"Anything else?"

"I had them get in touch with their commander of the oval craft—while they were under strict guard, of course. I had them report about their unsuccessful invasion attempt. Marshall tuned in to their telepathic conversation. He could understand everything. Their commander ordered the two prisoners to set themselves free at once. When they informed him that they could not obey his orders because of their hypnotic trance, he instructed them to commit suicide. I countermanded this order immediately to prevent them from destroying themselves. This way, at least I still managed to find out that their oval shaped spaceship has landed somewhere on the moon, where it intends to remain. The M.S. plan to wait there for the arrival of reinforcements. In my opinion it is senseless to start searching for them on the moon. If they are cautious and avoid exposing themselves to attack, we will never succeed in ferreting them out. But we must forever remain on guard and never relax our precautions against their threat, although I believe that for the time being there is no imminent danger of invasion."

"This is probably nothing but the lull before the storm,"

warned Bell. He was obviously not satisfied with the outcome of the battle. The enemy had not been totally defeated. "Someday they will try to get even with us."

"By then our defensive weapons will have been perfected and we will have evolved better tactics still. Don't worry, Reg. Ellert has shown us the right way to deal with them. The main thing we have to remember is, whenever we encounter a Mind Snatcher in his natural body, we must not hesitate an instant before we destroy it."

This remark evidently upset Bell. He inquired anxiously, "And how about our two prisoners here? Who is supposed to execute them?"

Rhodan smiled grimly. "I only temporarily prevented the two M.S. from carrying out their commander's order to commit suicide. As soon as I had completed my cross-examination of both prisoners I released them from my hypnotic influence."

"So?"

"They finally obeyed their commander's orders, without hesitation. You know, it's most interesting how they resemble wasps in this respect. They too have horrible poisonous stingers."

Only the most urgent circumstances could bring Allan D. Mercant to leave his underground fortress under the Greenland ice cap. Even then he would do so only very reluctantly—particularly since these sorties were brought about by unpleasant events.

This time, though, Mercant had a feeling as if he were going on vacation. He clambered into his small, fast service plane and ordered the pilot to fly to New York. The sensation of freedom stayed with Mercant as he walked up Fifth Avenue. Suddenly he stopped and looked across the street to a twenty-two story building.

Between the seventh and ninth floors he observed the giant letters G.C.C. This then must be where the General Cosmic Company had its offices! Mercant felt a bit disappointed. He had expected that Rhodan would have bought up at least the whole skyscraper. But maybe, Mercant thought, his own lack of experience in business matters did not permit him to make a proper judgment of what course Rhodan should have taken in this respect.

As Mercant was riding up in the elevator, his happy feeling gave way to a queasy sensation in his stomach. He realized once again that he had to carry all the responsibility on his own shoulders. Deep inside he knew that he was on Rhodan's side, shared his goals and principles. But his own position with the government forced him to pay a professional visit to the offices of the G.C.C. He was unhappy to have to obey the call of duty, which forced him to spy on his friends.

He almost changed his mind about his official mission when Miss Lawrence, the receptionist, welcomed him with a friendly smile that spoke of her pleasure at his unexpected visit. But then Mercant remembered that the success of his action depended solely on him. If things did not go according to plan or if they went too much against his grain, he would simply tell Homer G. Adams the plain truth. Or better still, he would tell it directly to Perry Rhodan himself.

The short, slight manager of the mighty concern received Mercant with extreme politeness. No one could have guessed by looking at him that not too long ago he had been released from a prison in England, where he had spent fourteen years for embezzling large sums of money.

The two men shook hands and sat down in comfortable leather chairs. Mercant accepted a cigar from Adams, although he really could not stand their stench. Homer leaned back, contentedly puffing away.

"And to what do I owe the pleasure of this unexpected visit, Mr. Mercant? Did the Chief send you?"

He was getting at three things simultaneously, thought Mercant, admiring Adams's skill. First he had asked the reason for this visit. At the same time he had expressed his consternation that Mercant had failed to inform him about his intended call. And to top it off, the catch question, whether Rhodan knew about this meeting. It was obvious that Rhodan would have let Adams know about such a conference if he had any idea about it. Mercant felt he would have to proceed very cautiously not to fall into some trap.

"No, Rhodan knows nothing about this visit," Mercant replied truthfully. "I come on behalf of my own government to obtain certain information." Much better in any case to place his cards on the table. After all, there was no longer a state of war between the government of the Western Bloc and Perry Rhodan. "It is concerning the construction of our common space fleet."

Homer fingered his rimless glasses, which gave him a very old fashioned appearance. "The space fleet? Hasn't that topic been sufficiently discussed by our experts? To be honest with you, Mr. Mercant, I don't understand too much of what it's all about. I am interested only in the financial aspect of the whole project."

"I haven't come here to bother you with the technical details about the hypothetical propulsion." Mercant smiled patiently. "I am not at all interested in that. Besides, I don't understand any more about it than you do. As you probably know, my government made a first contribution of eighteen billion dollars. How much did you receive from the other governments?"

Homer raised his eyebrows. "The total sum amounts to seventy billion dollars," he said as if he were speaking of seventy cents.

"So much? We did not count on such a huge sum."

"Neither did I," Homer admitted frankly. "In any case, the project is already in full swing. New factories and production complexes are rising all over the world. Our most capable men are working day and night—that means the people from the Western, Eastern, and Asiatic blocs. For the first time in human history the inhabitants of this planet are collaborating on a common task. We have learned from the successfully averted invasion of the insect race how important such a collaboration has become for mankind. Anyone who secretly pursued any egotistic nationalistic goals would be committing a crime against humanity."

Mercant could not help but feel that Homer had his own private reasons for making such a long speech. But he did not give himself away by revealing how he felt. He simply nodded his head in agreement.

"You are so right, Mr. Adams. But I can hardly believe that anybody could harbor such a thought nowadays."

"I wouldn't be so sure, Mr. Mercant," interrupted Adams. "Just a few days ago they caught a Western spy in one of the Chinese industrial concerns. I cannot believe that this guy was carrying on there out of his own free will."

Mercant folded his hands in a nervous gesture. He shook his head. "If you deal with such a huge organization as that of the Western Defense, it takes a long time before they can call back all their agents. Most of our people are working on their own most of the time. Quite often we don't even know where they are at the moment—"

"But wouldn't it be wiser to avoid such incidents totally in the interests of world cooperation?" Homer interrupted rather rudely. "It doesn't take much—just some such stupid thing could disrupt the newly established unity among the nations of this world. Anyhow, it will be many years before the last trace of distrust has disappeared. I know, Mercant, that you are on our side; but you should get rid of the last ties that bind you to a cause that forces you to actions running contrary to your own convictions. Do you get what I mean?"

Mercant raised his hands in a little gesture of regret. "I certainly understand you, Adams. I have already discussed this previously with Rhodan. He is of the opinion, though, that I should remain working for the Western Powers. After all, we can't know who would take my place once I leave my position. This way seems to be the lesser evil."

"You have a point there," admitted Homer. "But let's go on with our talk. We are sending orders all over the world from our scientific center. Parts of our future space fleet are already being manufactured in several large industrial concerns. Mankind is already constructing the most advanced weapons bit by bit, without realizing what all the single parts will become once they are properly assembled. So far they seem like incomprehensible fragments, which do not reveal what the end product might be. And it is the same way with our spaceships. In another six months we will have reached the point where we can assemble ten faster than light space cruisers within a few days from all the individual segments that different factories have turned out independently from each other, without knowing what all was for. You see what undreamed of potential can be put into reality by mankind once they forget their differences. Of course, the world does not have any idea about all this, and it might be wise to keep this information to yourself for the time being."

Adams watched Mercant's reaction to what he just had said. Homer's foxy eyes sparkled amusedly behind his thick glasses. He seemed to be aware of the dilemma into which his words had plunged Allan D. Mercant. To make matters even worse, Adams seemed to enjoy thoroughly the secret pleasure that this knowledge afforded him.

"In addition to all that, we are supplying all the tool machines unknown to man," he continued with apparent unconcern, thus giving Mercant all the information he had believed he could obtain only with the greatest of difficulties. "These tool machines have been built in other parts of the world under our supervision, according to plans supplied by us. We also give them all kinds of materials that Rhodan has brought down to Earth from the moon. As you probably know, only the exterior of the Arkonide research craft, stranded on the moon, was destroyed when bombed by hostile terrestrial military forces. The interior with its huge storerooms remained mainly undamaged, with all the technical secrets of the Arkonide supertechnology intact."

Once again Mercant nodded his head vigorously to express his agreement with what Adams was telling him. The little financial wizard had just put his finger right on the spot. There were incredible treasures hidden up there in the remains of the wrecked Arkonide spaceship. But the Western Bloc did not possess a single spacecraft suitable to get at this treasure trove.

Or perhaps . . . ?

There had been feverish activity of late at Nevada Spaceport; Mercant was well informed about this. But for the first time Mercant's men had been refused admission to the assembly halls inside the industrial plant. Something was going on there that the world should not know about.

All of a sudden it seemed to Mercant that his eyes had been opened. Everything fell into place. He compared his mission to obtain information that appeared so harmless on the surface with what he just had learned from Adams. Then it became clear to him that the government of the Western Bloc was not strictly living up to its agreements with Perry Rhodan.

Mercant was furious. His anger was based on his innate honesty. But before he could speak up, the manager of the G.C.C. continued, "What else were you supposed to find out from me, Mercant?"

An embarrassed smile came over the boyish face of the Chief of the Western Defense. "We were only interested in the bit about the cruiser on the moon. All the other questions were intended as diversionary tactics."

"Thanks," countered Adams. "I knew that all along. Why do they want to find out all this?"

"I wouldn't have the faintest idea," Mercant said frankly. "I just noticed the possibility of certain coincidences, but I am not yet quite sure. But you may rest assured that I will inform Rhodan without fail if I have the slightest proof for a certain suspicion that just has occurred to me. By the way, many thanks for your sincerity and frankness. Believe me, my superiors will learn only whatever I think they should about this conversation."

"You can always count on me, Mercant," replied Adams, and rose to see his caller to the door. Then Homer returned to his seat and stared for a few seconds at the telecom that would permit instant communication with Rhodan in his desert base or anywhere else he might be.

But then Adams shook his head. Rhodan had more important things to do than being bothered with suspicions. For the time being it would be sufficient if Adams kept an eye on this affair.

General Pounder walked leisurely across the Nevada Spaceport testing grounds in company of Lieutenant Colonel Maurice. They were approaching one of the many giant halls that lay row on row under the burning midday sun.

This was the place where a few years ago the *Stardust I* had been built, the ship had taken Rhodan and his crew on the first successful flight to the moon; and here too had been constructed the moon rocket that sometime later was sent up to the moon to destroy the stranded Arkonide cruiser, whereby both attacker and attacked perished.

The huge hangarlike hall had no windows, in contrast to the neighboring sheds, which reminded one of hothouses, with entire walls and roofs made of glass. This building seemed hermetically sealed from the outside world, while its neighbors let in freely the plentiful sunshine.

The general pounded the small entrance door with his

mighty fists. A tiny crack opened, and a face became visible that examined the general from head to toe, as if he had never seen him before.

"What do you want?" inquired the man inside the door.

"I am General Pounder," answered the general. "I want to get in!"

"I'm afraid that's not possible. Against regulations."

"Whose?"

"General Pounder's orders, sir."

Lieutenant Maurice burst out laughing, while Pounder's face grew as red as a beet. The door opened a bit more and a young man in uniform became visible. He saluted smartly as if wanting to apologize for his illogical but militarily correct behavior.

"I must examine your passes," he added, strictly according to the prescribed rules and regulations."

Pounder looked at Maurice, who at once stopped laughing.

"You see, Maurice, that's the way our soldiers should be trained. I hope you did not forget your identity card. Otherwise, I can't take you inside with me."

Fortunately both officers had their papers with them. The young guard examined them thoroughly, before he opened the door sufficiently to permit the two to enter the shed. Once inside General Pounder and Lieutenant Colonel Maurice had to close their eyes. The light was blinding.

There were no partitions whatsoever in the immense hall, which stretched for more than six hundred feet in length and up to a height of more than one hundred fifty feet. A maze of scaffolding and cranes made easily accessible every corner of the huge building. Little trains moved along shiny rails toward a tunnel, disappearing in its depth, not to be seen again.

A feverish activity reigned inside the shed, and the din of the machines was deafening. Lieutenant Colonel Maurice clapped his hands over his ears to protect them from the sudden onslaught of unbearable noise.

"I can't hear myself think," he shouted to the general.

"What did you say?"

"I was only saying that it's too noisy in here for talking to each other."

General Pounder shook his head and pointed to his ears.

"I can't understand a word you are saying!" he roared.

Lieutenant Colonel Maurice threw his hands up in despair. Then he laughed. He knew it made no sense even to attempt to explain that the noise was too great here in this shed.

Workers were rushing past them, never giving them so much as a glance. Highly polished metal parts glided past on low trains, disappearing in the small work sheds that ringed the free space in the center of the huge hall. This was where the engineers had their offices.

General Pounder stopped suddenly. He had taken his assistant along today for the first time inside the heavily guarded work shed, which was controlled day and night by a cordon of soldiers. Lieutenant Colonel Maurice stepped aside for a moment to let pass a worker and then looked up. He was thunderstruck! For there, right in the middle of the hall, resting on a flat ramp that slanted slightly upward, he saw a long silvery torpedo. Round portholes extended along the center line and a small crane was just depositing a cylindrical tank inside the loading hatch of the storeroom.

The noise of the riveters' guns drowned out Maurice's curse.

There in front of him, barely fifty feet away, lay the exact replica of the *Stardust I*, which once had carried Perry Rhodan and his men to their first landing on the moon.

And no one in the outside world had any idea of the existence of this new space rocket. . . .

Three months went by before Perry Rhodan felt certain that the Mind Snatchers would not risk another invasion, for the time being, at least. During these three months he had almost managed to forget them, since the whole world was under the spell of the General Cosmic Company. Everywhere on Earth mighty industrial complexes had sprung up, where production was started under the direction of the technicians and planners.

Homer G. Adams sat in his offices in New York like a giant spider in its web. The walls were covered with maps, dotted with tiny flags with incomprehensible letters and signs. Homer spent all his time in front of the telecom. Occasionally he got some sleep.

The power of the concern he had built up grew from day to day. The day when a certain Benjamin Wilder could proclaim that the world was his, because he had financed it, seemed close at hand. Benjamin Wilder was the power behind G.C.C., and hardly anyone knew that Benjamin Wilder was just another alias for Perry Rhodan.

Khrest failed to understand this phenomenon of practically runaway development. It was alien to his way of thinking. He had underestimated the dynamics of human nature, although he believed humans to be the most capable race the Arkonides had ever encountered in the universe. Silently he walked alongside Rhodan as they left their living quarters shortly before sunset in order to get some fresh air. Reginald joined them.

Instinctively the three went in the direction of that three sided pyramid under which the body of a man was waiting to be awakened to life again.

They were still at quite some distance from the mausoleum that housed Ernst Ellert's lifeless form, when they recognized a tall, slender figure standing in front of the structure.

Perry Rhodan could not hide his surprise as he called out to his friends, "It's Thora! What is she doing out here?"

The trio approached the un-Earthly beautiful Arkonide woman, who stood there looking at them intently. Her eyes met Rhodan's, and for the first time he failed to detect her usual derision and scorn. On the contrary, there was a hesitant question in her expression. A wave of strange emotions flowed from her lovely features, but they revealed nothing negative.

She was the first to break the silence after the three men had come close to where she waited for them. "It is strange that we meet out here, but maybe it is not just by accident. Don't you sometimes have the impression that Ellert is still somehow among us, even if our senses cannot perceive him?"

Rhodan was amazed; it was more than mysterious that she should have experienced the same feeling he did. Once, Bell had remarked that Ellert's mind might have lost its ability to return to his body and that his spirit might now be wandering about aimlessly in the present time. However, Rhodan and Khrest were of the opinion that Ellert's mind, if it still possessed a consciousness of its own, was no longer residing in the present. When Ellert was attempting to escape from physical death, the electro shock had driven his mind into another dimension, from where there was no way back. Whether this dimension meant the past, the present, or the future was impossible for them to guess. But if it had really been in the present time, then Ellert should have been able to establish some communication with them, somehow using the mutants as his mouthpiece.

"He is still living in our emotions, Thora," Rhodan replied calmly. "Someday in the future we might catch up with him, if he hasn't traveled too far ahead of us on the time stream. By the way, why should you be so interested in Ellert's fate? He was nothing but an Earthling."

She tried to hide her embarrassment. "Truly intelligent races have the privilege of admitting that they have made mistakes. The Arkonides *are* intelligent. Therefore, I am acting according to my intellectual level when I admit having underestimated the inhabitants of this planet. But this does not mean, on the other hand, that I consider them our equals."

"No one would ask you to do that—at least, not yet," Rhodan said with sincerity. "We have won a great deal already if you have been able to revise your former hostile attitude. It is a fact that we have overcome a common enemy through our concerted efforts. That has created a link between us, Thora!"

Khrest stepped closer to Thora. He gazed into her golden eyes, and a gentle smile lit up his ascetic features. "Thank you, Thora, for these words! They are like a golden bridge over which someday in the far future the only path will lead that will bring about the survival of the realm of our galactic empire. It is possible that Rhodan, too, will have to walk across that bridge in the future."

"I wouldn't mind joining you, if that bridge is made of gold," said Bell without a trace of pathos. "The only question is whether I will live that long."

"There is no reason why we could not continue our research project with the *Good Hope*," replied Khrest. "We no longer have the big space cruiser with which we started our expedition to find the planet of eternal life, but the *Good Hope* is big enough to take us there, even if it is not powerful enough to carry us back to our home planet."

There was a long pause. Then Rhodan shook his head. "There are more urgent tasks at hand right now, I am sorry to say. We must first train our mutants, and I want to establish a base on Venus for that purpose. In a few days I will fly to Venus and prepare the first camp for our mutant school. As far as we have been able to tell from our observations of the planet, there is no intelligent life on Venus. Later on, when peace and order have been firmly established here on this globe, we will have plenty of time to start the search for the planet of eternal life. But to be honest with you, I sincerely doubt that our efforts will meet with success."

"We will find that planet!" shouted Thora. "It *does* exist!" There was an almost fanatical fire of enthusiasm burning in her eyes. "We were told so by some expeditions that have returned from there. But they guard the secret so jealously that it will mean bitter battles once we reach the planet that will give us immortality."

Rhodan smiled.

"I'll believe it when I see it!"

Bell joined the conversation. "Wouldn't it be wonderful if we could finally get rid of having to be afraid of our own funerals? Look at all the survivor benefits I could collect from all my friends!"

No one laughed at Bell's suggestion, and he turned away, a bit insulted at his friends' lack of appreciation for his peculiar brand of humor. He contemplated the pyramid tomb, which the rays of the setting sun had turned into a luminous golden hue.

Perry stepped over to Khrest and Thora and held out his hand to her. "Are we going to be friends from now on?" he inquired, a bit unsure of himself.

For an instant the customary arrogance flitted across her face, but then she shook Rhodan's hand. "I both admire and fear you, Perry Rhodan. But you will understand that such feelings do not engender any true friendship. I also realize that we depend on you and that we must cooperate with each other. Should *that* be the basis of a genuine friendship? Besides, Khrest forces me to be cooperative. You see, I accept your hand here only because I must do so. Are you satisfied with that?"

"Yes, for the time being," said Rhodan. "Sometime in the future you will give me your hand, but then you will do it for different reasons. Till that time comes, I will have to be satisfied with what I have here. Yes, I am quite happy. May I thank you for it, Thora?"

For a moment their eyes fused and their hands joined, making them as one. It might have been quite a solemn moment if Bell had not chosen to sigh deeply and interrupt with his blessing: "Amen."

The most solemn of all words deprived the pact between the man and the woman of any solemnity. Maybe because this word had been uttered by Bell.

The sun sank below the horizon, and suddenly the monument lost its luminous glow. It was as if an invisible flame had been extinguished inside the metal of which the pyramid had been constructed.

The first star came up in the sky.

Without knowing why, Perry Rhodan saw in this some inner connection that promised an optimistic prognosis for the farthest future. . . .

BASE ON VENUS

CHAPTER ONE

The desert had not known such activity since the hordes of Gengis Khan had swept from there to the west seven hundred years before.

The Arkonide worker robots, together with the engineers and specialists that had come here from all the corners of the Earth, were busy constructing the huge industrial complex that Rhodan had envisioned as the nucleus of his future capital of the Third Power. This was the center of production of the space fleet, which alone could guarantee the safety of this remote region' of the galaxy. The work progressed at a very satisfactory pace.

Time was in his favor, Rhodan tried to convince himself. Finally, the great powers of the world had come to accept the existence of his tiny but vitally important state; his victory over the Fantan people had earned him the gratitude of the other nations. Rhodan was confident he would be able to keep the dreaded insectlike Mind Snatchers at bay, at least for the time being.

But these two alien invaders had surely been just the avant garde of the many hostile races from outer space who were bound to be attracted to this corner of the universe by the distress signals of the destroyed Arkonide cruiser on the moon. The little time that was left to mankind had to be used wisely in preparing themselves for the expected onslaught.

It would take them at least two to three years, thought Rhodan, who fervently hoped for such a breathing spell. Then they would no longer have to live in constant fear of an invasion threat.

Rhodan had been under constant pressure lately. Too many urgently pressing tasks needed his immediate attention. His thoughts were in one continuous uproar. He could almost sympathize with the amazement with which the alien Khrest regarded the feverish activity that had mushroomed around the shores of the Goshun salt lake.

It seemed hard to believe that so few men had accomplished so much in such a short time. But then, they had had the advantage of the accumulated scientific knowledge that the two Arkonide survivors were sharing with them.

"We shouldn't delay any longer!" urged Reginald Bell. "We must have some secondary base—it's vitally important for us!"

Perry Rhodan calmed his friend with a reassuring slap on the shoulder. "We are leaving in two hours."

"Great! What are your plans?"

"We'll first fly to the moon. We'll salvage whatever we can from the wrecked Arkonide cruiser. There are still quite a few things in it we can use. From there we will proceed straight to Venus."

Rhodan stopped and pondered for a moment. "You are right, Reg. We need a secondary base more than anything else at the present."

Whatever precautions they might take on Earth, there was no absolutely safe place in the whole world should the invading aliens suddenly overpower them. It was too great a risk, for all mankind might be annihilated. Therefore, he *must* establish an outpost on Venus. Though this might not save Earth from total destruction, it would still guarantee the survival of a few members of the human race somewhere else in a safe spot. Thus, the holocaust would not be the end of the human species.

Khrest fully approved of Rhodan's plan. "I can't help but admire your drive and decisiveness, Rhodan. How lucky for our weary Arkonide forces to have found such a vital young ally. Whatever fate has in store for our galactic empire, we could not have wished for a better solution."

Thora did not share Khrest's enthusiasm. She still kept vacillating between her intuitive distrust of the Earthlings and what her reasoning mind advised her to admit. Long term prejudices were difficult to uproot, even in the most brilliant being. She still considered man as far inferior to her own race, not worthy to be treated as an equal. Perry

Rhodan was probably the only exception she was willing to make in this respect.

The *Good Hope* took off at dusk.

Rhodan was starting from his home planet with the comfortable knowledge that he had left everything behind in the most capable hands. He was accompanied by Tako Kakuta, the Japanese telepath, who had passed command of the mutant corps temporarily over to Ras Tschubai, his African counterpart. Little Betty Toufry, whose amazing telepathic and telekinetic powers made her a valuable ally, would assist Ras in his continued search against possible M.S. intruders. And if worse should come to worst, it would be comparatively easy for the *Good Hope* to interrupt her mission and return home in practically no time.

Once again Rhodan's thoughts turned to the strange fate that had befallen Ernst Ellert. Fury and anger welled up in Rhodan whenever he was reminded of the loss of his most valuable mutant. He had possessed the unique gift of teletemporation, as Rhodan had characterized the ability that the more prosaic Bell had called "letting his mind take a walk anywhere along the time track."

Ellert was apparently dead, and all hope had died with him. Sometimes it seemed to Rhodan as if Nature had followed the dictates of some mysterious law and tried to correct a horrible mistake she had made by eradicating the monster she had created. Ellert seemed to defy all laws of the universe; he was far more strange than the frightful Mind Snatchers, who had come wanting to destroy the Earth.

Rhodan moved his hand across his forehead as if trying to wipe away the thoughts that had preoccupied him during the automatically controlled moon flight of the *Good Hope*. Now they were preparing for the landing. The *Good Hope* had completed a partial orbit around the moon and was now approaching the scattered wreckage of the destroyed Arkonide cruiser, whose radioactivity had fallen to almost negligible levels and no longer constituted any danger to the crew.

Rhodan had visited the wreck several times since it had been exploded by several powerful H-bombs of terrestrial origin. He had come to search for any remains that could still be put to use. There had never been any unforeseen incidents. The moon was a dead world, as it had been since time immemorial.

Therefore, it caused quite a sensation when suddenly the shrill signal of the detector sounded out loud.

"Unidentified object at phi zero five, theta three three six!" announced Bell. "On the surface of the moon. No movement discernible."

Rhodan bent over the picture screen, searching for the coordinates given by Bell. The object was miserably small, nothing but a glittering fleck of light on the dull surface of the dead world of the moon.

Rhodan switched off the automatic pilot and began to guide the ship manually, while continuing their descent to the moon, now at reduced speed. He depressed a button of the intercom.

"Eric, we have spotted something down below. Contact it by shortwave radio and let me know if you get an answer! Bell will give you the coordinates."

A little while later the doctor came on over the telecom. "I can't get an answer from that thing down there."

"Keep trying. We are descending!" replied Rhodan.

The spacecraft executed a wide loop above the expanse of wreckage below, approaching it now from a different direction, while descending to an altitude of fifty miles. The board telescope should be able by now to enlarge the object sufficiently so that it could be identified.

Could this be a vehicle of the Mind Snatchers? Rhodan found this implausible. It would be contrary to the wiliness of the M.S. to leave something so conspicuous lying out in the open, where sooner or later a terrestrial spaceship might come to investigate.

Could it be a trap?

Rhodan turned to Thora. "Be ready to open fire!"

Thora walked over to the control panel whose buttons were connected with all the armament that the *Good Hope* carried on board. The ship now hovered vertically above the glittering object on the ground.

"Bell, what can you make out on the telescope?"

Bell had adjusted the telescope so that it projected an image on one of the picture screens. "For heaven's sake!" he groaned. "It's a rocket. Just like our *Stardust!*"

"We are going to land now!" said Rhodan.

"Wait!" yelled Bell.

Rhodan stopped his hand in midair, as he was just about to pull a lever to execute the landing maneuver. All eyes turned to the microwave detector where the strange rocket appeared as a bright dash. Two tiny white specks had detached themselves from it and were traveling with amazing speed toward the center of the screen.

Bell's eyes threatened to pop out of their sockets. "But that can't be! They are shooting at us!"

A few hours earlier the following events had taken place.

The *Greyhound*, a rocketship of the *Stardust* type, which had been built secretly at the Nevada Spaceport facilities as a last attempt to break the supremacy of the Third Power, had set out to the moon, where the Western Powers hoped to find material in the destroyed Arkonide cruiser. With this they intended to bridge the gap between their own lagging technology and the monopoly of the Arkonides' far advanced state of science enjoyed by Rhodan's new realm.

The landing maneuver on the moon turned out to be the most difficult phase of the *Greyhound*'s secretive mission. At first the spaceship had been guided by precise impulses sent from the ground station, and the automatically controlled flight had been uneventful. But now the *Greyhound* was above the landing site, which was on the other side of the moon. The craft was therefore cut off from the automatic guidance signals coming from Earth. It would take all the skill of the two pilots to carry out the landing for which they had been specially trained back on Earth.

The two pilots, Lieutenant Colonel Michael Freyt and Lieutenant Conrad Derringhouse, formed the crew of the *Greyhound*, together with Captain Rod Nyssen, the gunner, and Major William Sheldon, in charge of the special duties connected with the salvage operations of the Arkonide material from the wrecked cruiser.

"Speed zero except for vertical descent," announced Derringhouse.

"Vertical speed thirty feet per second, constant," replied Lieutenant Colonel Freyt. "We are floating down like a feather!"

Freyt was a product of the same training school Perry

Rhodan had attended a few years earlier. They seemed almost like brothers. Tall, lean, serious, but with tiny crow's feet at the corners of their eyes that spoke of their tremendous sense of humor.

Both pilots were wearing their space suits but had pushed back their helmets far enough to be able to converse directly without the help of microphones. Nyssen and Sheldon, though, had their head gear all ready like the rest of their outfit. They could have stepped out onto the surface of the moon at any moment.

"Altitude twelve thousand feet!" signaled Derringhouse. His face bore the impish expression of a schoolboy playing hookey.

"Keep on braking!" ordered Freyt.

A surge of slightly increased speed coursed through the craft. Seconds later the effect of the weak lunar gravitational pull was felt again.

"Vertical speed eighteen feet per second. Distance, please!"

"Ten thousand feet, sir!"

Freyt was pleased. The landing maneuver was proceeding according to plan. If everything kept going as smoothly as until now, they would complete touchdown in another ten minutes and their mission would be accomplished.

Freyt was most eager to carry out his orders, although he did not approve of the motivation that had brought about this mission. Sometime back he had been part of the attacking forces that had kept up a constant barrage against the huge energy barrier surrounding the tiny desert base of the young Third Power. In the meantime, though, he had come to believe that no other power on Earth was entitled to help itself to the Arkonide treasures, particularly behind Rhodan's back.

Despite his moral objections he had accepted the mission. After all, he was a military man, used to obeying orders. And besides, his instructions precluded any hostile confrontation should he ever come face to face with Rhodan's forces on the moon.

"Altitude?"

"Five thousand feet."

The surface of the moon looked like a shallow dish into which the *Greyhound* kept sinking lower and lower. Freyt and his crew had been warned about this optical illusion that would surprise the astronauts when landing on a relatively small celestial body.

The ground at the projected landing site appeared smooth and even but Freyt did not rely on mere visual observation. Derringhouse, who kept checking the distance from the moon's surface, was at the same time operating a device that could distinguish slight irregularities at ground zero, once they had come as close as three thousand feet. The *Greyhound* had been equipped, like the *Stardust* before her, with hydromechanical landing supports that could easily adjust for deviations ranging from nine to twenty feet.

"What does it look like down below?" inquired Freyt.

"So far so good. Soil irregularities up to twelve feet; that's all."

"How far away are we?"

"Eighteen hundred feet, sir."

"Let me know when we reach one thousand feet. Then we'll brake once more."

The two pilots closed their helmets. Conversation was possible now only via throat mike.

"One thousand feet, sir," came Derringhouse's announcement.

"Watch out! Brakes!" came Freyt's echo at once.

A new jolt coursed through the *Greyhound.*

"Six hundred feet!" came Derringhouse's voice over the space helmet intercom. "Ground irregularities not exceeding three feet."

The seconds moved at snail's pace. Derringhouse began to count. "Two hundred feet . . . one eighty feet . . . one fifty feet . . . one twenty feet . . ."

"Check for ground irregularities!" called Freyt.

"None over two feet, sir," answered Derringhouse, and continued counting. "Sixty . . . thirty . . ." One minute later he yelled triumphantly, "The landing supports are touching ground! We've made it! Support B and C at the same level, support A at minus two feet."

"That's nothing. No need to—"

And then it came, a hard jolt that shook the rocket.

"A is sinking! Correction, sir!" shouted Derringhouse.

Freyt slammed down on the regulator button. Another jolt, while the B and C landing supports were trying to adjust for the difference. And still one more concussion.

"A keeps sinking!" yelled the lieutenant. "We are . . . The ground is giving way . . . a big crack!"

Dark crevices now became visible on the ground, giving way under the weight of the rocket. The cracks kept widening as the *Greyhound* sank in deeper and deeper.

"Look out!" barked Freyt. "Full speed ahead now!"

Derringhouse jerked back into his seat. Freyt grabbed the lever and pulled it back. The *Greyhound* began to lean over at a steep angle, reacting to the thrust of the jets.

Derringhouse stared wide eyed at the screen. "Stop it!" he screamed.

Freyt released the lever.

"Watch out! We are toppling over!"

Landing support A snapped off abruptly, and the slender rocket crashed to the ground. A heavy piece of machinery tore loose from its wall clamps and shot like a giant bullet through the cabin floor and out through the craft's hull. The air from inside the cabin escaped through the hole with a hissing noise.

Freyt heard someone cry out. He waited for the final explosion of the rocket, which he subconsciously feared was unavoidable.

A minute went by. Nothing happened. Freyt opened his eyes, which he had closed expecting death. He sat up, unable to still believe he had survived this disaster. Inside the cabin, utter confusion reigned. Broken instruments, crumpled walls, motionless bodies were all enveloped in a cloud of moon dust that had penetrated through the torn hull.

"Derringhouse!" Freyt called out anxiously. "Nyssen! Sheldon!"

Somebody was moaning.

"I am still in one piece," came Nyssen's half choked voice.

"Where are you? Where are the others?"

"I don't know. Wait a second till I get myself untangled here."

From beneath the wreckage, Nyssen's fishbowl shaped helmet emerged.

"Just look at that mess!"

Freyt had managed in the meantime to extricate himself from the debris. "Nyssen, help me here, will you!"

Together they cleared away some of the shattered pieces of machinery that completely filled the back of the room.

Nyssen grasped the leg of a space suit. "Looks like our lieutenant."

They pulled him out. Apparently he had been thrown out of his chair by the impact, which had also rendered him unconscious. He was breathing heavily.

"Let's go on!"

They pushed aside some more bits of wreckage. That's when they found Sheldon. At first they thought he had only fainted. But when they turned him around, they discovered a large tear in his space suit. It was torn from the right shoulder down to his left hip. Freyt straightened out. He looked pale. Nyssen mumbled, "Sorry, pal. What a shame to lose you, Sheldon!"

"Keep an eye on Derringhouse while I crawl out here through the passage to the airlock and inspect the rest of the ship," said Freyt.

When he returned Derringhouse had just regained consciousness.

"How do you feel? Can you move all right?" asked Nyssen. He helped his friend to stand up.

Derringhouse gingerly felt himself all over, flexing his arms and legs. "Nothing broken, it seems, just a few bumps."

"Well then, let's get on with the job. Work is the best cure."

Feverishly they began to take stock of their situation. "Radio transmitter and receiver gone!"

"Reactor electronic disrupted!"

"Emergency power supply intact!"

And finally Nyssen's triumphant voice, "Armament undamaged!"

Freyt found their food supply in good order. He also discovered an emergency store of oxygen, sufficient to fill one room of the *Greyhound,* if there was one left without cracks or holes in its walls.

The reactors did not respond, although they knew it would be possible to repair the damage. Still, it made no sense even to attempt this, since they were unable to raise the rocket to an upright position.

They climbed outside. The exterior wall was partially

caved in, and torn in some places. The spot where landing support A was supposed to have found a firm foothold was nothing but a gaping hole whose rims were only a couple of inches thick.

Nyssen regarded the caved-in moon surface at this spot with obvious disgust while cursing softly to himself.

"We are equipped for a two week stay here on the moon," Freyt stated calmly. "Not before another twenty days will the people on Earth become alarmed and start rescue operations. We won't last that long. So let's—"

"Sir, over there!" exclaimed Derringhouse, pointing to the sky. Freyt shot around. With narrowed eyes he could make out a glimmering dot up in the dark firmament. The dot approached rapidly.

"The aliens!" cried Nyssen.

"Which aliens?"

"The Mind Snatchers! Those damned insects!"

Freyt hesitated a moment. Then he commanded, "Nyssen, man the guns. But don't shoot unless I give you the order! You, Conrad, stay here outside with me!"

Nyssen climbed back into the *Greyhound,* while Freyt and Derringhouse did not take their eyes off the scintillating flash in the sky.

The object passed high above the wrecked rocket and returned in a wide loop. Now they were immediately overhead.

"They are descending," observed the lieutenant.

"What's their altitude, Nyssen?"

"If my instruments are still correct, about fifty miles."

"How many missiles can you dispatch at a time?"

"Two, sir."

"Go ahead, fire!"

The torpedo tubes of the fighter projectiles had settled at the same horizontal position as the whole *Greyhound.* The lunar ground trembled, and the wreck tilted slightly on its side as Nyssen let go. But despite the unfavorable initial direction, both missiles climbed up to the sky searching out their target.

"That's obvious!" Rhodan answered curtly. "Either they have gone crazy or they—"

Out of the corner of his eye he had noticed Thora getting ready for action at the armament control panel. She seemed overeager. Rhodan spun around in midsentence.

"Thora!"

Thora hit a tumbler switch full force. Rhodan dived for her, but was too late. He grasped her roughly by her shoulders and flung her aside. With an angry cry she fell to the ground.

Rhodan flipped the switch back again.

"Reg! She used crystal field neutralization. The dot down there has disappeared."

Manoli's voice announced, "Ready for defense action!"

The two missiles had come close to the *Good Hope,* which was now surrounded by a protective energy barrier that deflected the projectiles, changing their course. They shot harmlessly off in a wide arc, missing the spacecraft, then disappearing in the vastness of space.

Slowly Thora got to her feet again.

"Don't you ever again forget to wait for my orders to start shooting! I'll hold you responsible if anything has happened to those people down there."

"Responsible for what?" She seemed to mock him. "They attacked us, and I simply had to defend ourselves."

"You knew they couldn't effectively attack us with their missiles. You are always ready to make fun of our underdeveloped technology, and now you pretend to feel threatened by it."

"They destroyed my cruiser!"

"Only because you were unable to defend it properly. Your crew was drugged with inertial" snapped Rhodan. "You knew perfectly well that our energy screen would protect us against any terrestrial weapons!"

Thora remained silent. Only the reddish glint flashing from behind her half closed eyelids revealed her emotions.

Rhodan turned away. His voice sounded weary as he announced, "We are landing."

"What's happening to the *Greyhound?*" Nyssen's shout startled Freyt and Derringhouse, who had intently followed the trajectory of their two missiles homing in on their target. The trio was prepared to see the explosion in the sky now at any moment. Turning their heads, they watched, the disaster that silently began to overtake their wrecked rocket ship.

Big chunks detached themselves from the hull and fell slowly toward the ground, turning to dust before they had reached the lunar soil. They had hardly realized what was going on before their ship was halfway dissolved.

"Oh no," moaned Freyt. "We have attacked the wrong people!"

For the military men on Earth knew well the kind of weapons the Arkonides had brought with them. Freyt could therefore easily identify the process by which the *Greyhound* was being destroyed. By applying an electric field whose microstructure imitated exactly that of the crystal lattice in which the molecules of solid matter were arranged, the crystal could be dissolved and the molecules set free. What remained was a thin gas composed of the same components as the solid body previously had been.

Head thrown back, Derringhouse observed the work of dissolution. The walls of the *Greyhound* crumbled until nothing was left of them. The whole process lasted about four to five seconds. The reactor, the jets, and the tanks began to slide and landed on the ground.

It dawned on Freyt that once they had fallen to the lunar surface, none of the parts were any longer under attack. Freyt realized this with a tremendous sense of relief.

"Nyssen!" the lieutenant colonel called with a faint voice that the captain could barely perceive. "Come here!"

Just at that moment a dark, voluminous shadow covered the sunlit plain. The lieutenant swung around with a cry filled with fear and almost stumbled to the ground.

But this was only the gigantic Arkonide space sphere, about to touch down.

Nyssen stood there overtaken by a sense of wonder as he watched the landing maneuver. He had seen the sphere once before, about nine months ago when he and Freyt had carried out the bombing attack against the Arkonide research cruiser, whose wreckage was now strewn over the ground. But at that time the distance between the two and the space sphere had been considerably greater.

"What a monster!" exclaimed the astonished Freyt. He

seemed to have recovered his composure. "Well! The only thing we can do now is to walk over to them and apologize for having attacked them by mistake!"

CHAPTER TWO

Rhodan saw the three men walk across the debris covered ground. The distance had shrunk to the point where they could already communicate via their space helmet intercom system.

"No foolishness now!" Rhodan ordered harshly.

"Don't worry, Rhodan," came Freyt's reply with reassuring swiftness. "What harm can you expect from three stranded astronauts?"

Rhodan recognized the voice. "Is that you, Michael Freyt? And who are the other two with you?"

"Captain Nyssen and Lieutenant Derringhouse."

"All right. You may board the ship."

Rhodan knew Nyssen, but he had never heard of Derringhouse. He turned around. Thora had jumped up in excitement. "Freyt!" she cried. "The Earthling who destroyed my cruiser!"

Rhodan interrupted her. "He did not do it on his own. He was only carrying out orders. You can't blame him exclusively for that attack."

Thora's eyes were spitting fire. "What do you plan to do with these people?"

"I'll take them aboard, of course. What else do you suggest?"

"That's out of the question! I won't permit this! I am the commander of the cruiser!"

"Which no longer exists!" Rhodan reminded her.

"The *Greyhound* is part of the cruiser. No difference whether it's the cruiser itself or its auxiliary vessel. I am commander of both! These two beasts can't come aboard!"

Thora was so enraged that she had not the least doubt that her words would end the argument between her and Rhodan. But there was an aftermath to this contest of wills. All who witnessed it knew that a decisive battle had taken place.

"Reg!" Rhodan spoke calmly to his friend. "Open the air lock!"

Thora had already walked over to her chair. At the sound of Rhodan's command she spun around. "But I have just told—"

"What you have to say is of no interest to me," snapped Rhodan.

Suddenly a painful groan came from Khrest, who had stayed in the background, resting on his couch.

"These three men will not step aboard my ship! Not under any circumstances!" shouted Thora in anger. "I believe to have made myself sufficiently clear on that point. I absolutely forbid—"

"You can't forbid anything here, Thora," Rhodan said gently.

The rest of Thora's words ended in a softly mumbled protest that soon died down entirely. Her shoulders began to droop in a gesture of utter defeat. Gently, Rhodan seized her by the arm, leading her out of the cabin.

Bell and Rhodan exchanged a swift glance of weary triumph.

A short while later the tall silhouette of Freyt came into view inside the doorway of the command center. He saluted. "You see before you a very remorseful man, sir," he told Rhodan. "I sincerely wish to apologize for the horrible blunder I committed."

"What blunder?"

"We mistook your craft for one of the invading Mind Snatchers' ships and tried to annihilate it."

"Why didn't you answer our calls?"

"We weren't even aware that you tried to contact us. Our rocket crash landed, and our communications system was destroyed."

"Why did you fly to the moon in the first place? What business have you here?"

Freyt contemplated the tip of his spaceboots.

"You can save your breath! I can imagine what brought you here!" thundered the infuriated Rhodan. "They sent you up here to ransack the wreckage, to see if you couldn't salvage some useful weapons for the NATO Command. That's it, Freyt!"

Freyt still remained silent.

Nyssen pushed his way past Freyt and planted himself in front of Rhodan. "Major Rhodan," he began, "you were once one of us. You graduated from the air force officers' training corps, when I had already made captain. Unfortunately—"

"Don't beat around the bush!"

Nyssen grinned. "You'll have to hear me out, whether you want it or not, the same as when you were nothing but a cadet. You know the regulations at the air force! We received orders to fly to the moon in order to rummage through the wrecked cruiser for anything that might be salvaged and come in useful for us. You should remember what would have happened to us if we had not obeyed at once."

"Yes, but you could have warned me at least," replied Rhodan.

Nyssen became serious and intent. In a subdued voice that barely concealed his emotions, he said sharply, "Not everyone can desert his own country and start running his own show."

Dead silence fell over the big command center. Everyone waited with bated breath for Rhodan's reaction.

Rhodan stood motionless like a statue. It was difficult to determine whether Nyssen's remark had really hit home. Finally he stepped forward and held out his hand to Nyssen. "Okay, Captain!" Rhodan smiled. "You have won!"

"How is she?"

"She is all right now," answered Khrest. "But if I were you I wouldn't try that again!"

Rhodan tried to defend himself. "I had no choice; I had to act this way."

Khrest explained, "You can't imagine the enormous energies hidden in her brain. I believe I am the only one who experienced the shock in its full extent, the same way she did. It felt as if someone attempted to sweep out the inside of my cranium with an iron broom!"

Khrest smiled as he continued. "You must have been absolutely furious at that moment, Perry! Just consider, though—our Arkonide brains might be better trained and more fully utilized than man's, but because of our general decay, our brains have become far less resistant than yours.

You can push Thora to the brink of insanity with such brutal attacks. I am quite serious, Perry!"

"I fully realize that, Khrest. This was exactly the reason why I was so harsh. At that moment, at least, it seemed the only method to bring Thora back to her senses. But you can rest assured, my friend, I won't repeat this shock treatment. There are other ways to control Thora's behavior."

Rhodan turned and walked down the corridor toward the command center. Khrest's eyes followed him. Unconsciously the Arkonide scientist imitated the proud posture of the Earthling. He straightened up his tired, drooping shoulders and held his head up high. Immediately he became aware of his unconscious action, and he smiled gently to himself.

Rhodan took the time to ascend sufficiently high in the *Good Hope* to reestablish radio communication with Washington, D.C. He had a long talk with the people whom he suspected had sent Freyt and his two friends on that fateful mission to the moon. Nobody, of course, would admit having been the instigator of that plan. They expressed sincere regret for this unfortunate incident. But Rhodan wanted more than mere excuses; he demanded certain compensations. His demands caused some consternation down in Washington, but they willingly acceded to his request.

At once Rhodan brought his ship down again to the lunar surface. Then he summoned the crew of the *Greyhound* to appear in the command center.

"I have just spoken with Washington. They apologized and have agreed to make reparations for their act of piracy. These are my terms, gentlemen!" Rhodan let his glance wander from Freyt to Nyssen and then on to Derringhouse, before he continued, "I want you to join my crew!"

Freyt narrowed his eyes; Derringhouse jumped halfway out of his seat. Only Nyssen remained calm. He was the first to speak up. "I have already stated my point of view."

Rhodan shook his head. "I am not asking you to desert to my side. I need three good astronauts, and you three would fill the bill. You have happened on to the scene at the right moment. If you should decide to join me, then the Space Command would give you an honorable discharge. I'll give you twenty-four hours to make up your minds. Thank you, gentlemen!"

Rhodan left the three space pilots. It took them exactly two hours to come to a decision. Their answer was "Yes."

The next four days were devoted to a thorough search of the wrecked Arkonide cruiser for anything worth salvaging.

The robot corps attached to the *Good Hope* cleared out the cruiser's interior cell, which had miraculously remained intact. There were more usable things than the *Good Hope* could transport in its storage compartments. Therefore, part of the recovered goods had to be stored on the moon for the time being. The robots erected a storage shed by using some of the metal sheeting of the cruiser's hull.

Rhodan made an inventory of the salvaged machinery and instruments. They consisted largely of consumer goods the Arkonides had used for intergalactic barter. Rhodan realized with a great sense of relief that this treasure trove would solve forever the financial worries of the young Third Power. He knew he could rely on Homer. G. Adams's financial skill to make the most advantageous use of the money they would obtain from the sale of these goods.

Rhodan reserved for his own use a series of automatic ray guns, portable nuclear energy weapons, and finally a complete plant for the manufacturing of special robots.

There was an additional gain that resulted from the salvage mission; it concerned Thora.

Rhodan had his own cabin on board the spacious *Good Hope*, as did all the other members of his crew. Twice already Thora had visited Rhodan in his own quarters, but several months had gone by since her last call. No wonder, therefore, that Rhodan was startled to find Thora in his cabin that evening. She was sitting comfortably relaxed in an armchair, waiting for him.

It was evening, according to Earth time. Outside, the rock strewn lunar ground was still bathed in sunlight, just as it had been just four days ago when the *Good Hope* had set down next to the wrecked *Greyhound*.

Thora apparently had not come to discuss the incident with the three terrestrial space pilots. She greeted Rhodan with a friendly smile. "I believe the time has come for us to establish a better relationship."

Rhodan could not conceal his astonishment. "This is exactly what I have been thinking for the past year, Thora. I am so glad that you have come to share my own opinion. What brought about this change of heart?"

"Reason seems to have won out finally."

Rhodan was puzzled. He could not quite believe that she had suddenly come to her senses after having displayed so much stubborn prejudice ever since they had met.

"Great! But what will that mean practically in our relationship?"

"I'll promise," Thora began in a timid voice, "no longer to challenge your authority as commander of this ship or any other vessel we build in the future."

"Thank you, Thora," Rhodan replied slowly. He tried to speak with warmth but failed, since his astonishment outweighed his feelings of gratitude. "On the other hand," he added after a while, "I depend on your judgment in many ways."

Thora smiled. "You don't need my advice, Perry! You know as much as any Arkonide astrocommander, including myself."

She was paying him compliments, thought Rhodan. She must have something up her sleeve.

Thora resumed the conversation. "Your next flight will take you to the planet you call Venus; isn't that so?"

"Why, of course, Thora." Rhodan was still puzzled. Every person on board the *Good Hope* had known the ultimate destination of their trip, even before they had left Earth.

"Will you be able to take along everything you salvaged from the wreck at once?"

"No. It will take us three trips."

"That's quite a while. Will it be safe for you to be absent from Earth that long?"

"Why not? Ras Tschubai is a most dependable fellow. If anything should go wrong, he'll contact me immediately."

Thora seemed to be searching for something suitable to say. Then she gave up the attempt. She rose and extended her hand, imitating the ways of the Earthlings she had so despised. "I hope this will be the beginning of our voluntary collaboration. Not because we are forced by necessity to work together, as until now, but because we both want to cooperate for our common good."

Shortly before the *Good Hope* took off for Venus, Rhodan had a talk with Khrest. He hoped in this way to find out something about what had motivated Thora's unexpected remarks. But when Rhodan sat across from Khrest, he did not know how to express what worried him.

He was so preoccupied by his thoughts that despite the mental block that shielded his mind from being probed by others, Khrest could read it like an open book. Nevertheless, Khrest preferred to approach the subject in a roundabout manner.

"Is there any possibility of repairing the inner cell of the wrecked cruiser so that it could be used again?" Khrest asked.

"You mean as a spaceship?"

Khrest nodded.

Rhodan immediately shook his head. "Impossible, Khrest. Nothing remained intact of the drive mechanism. The only thing we salvaged that might eventually help us rebuild the interstellar craft is the manufacturing plant for the specialized robots."

"How long will it take with their help?"

Rhodan shrugged. "A few years, I guess."

"Don't you see, Perry?"

"What am I supposed to see?"

Khrest answered with a sly smile. "I know somebody who clung with all her pride to the hope of being able to return to her home planet, Arkon, without having to take recourse to the aid of the primitive Earthlings. The moment this person realized that all such hope was lost, then . . well, you have witnessed yourself what happened!"

Rhodan understood. "You mean to say that all this time she was still clinging to the chance that her cruiser could be restored to working order?"

"Yes. And now she had to relinquish this dream. It can't be very easy for her. She needs a great deal of sympathy now."

"She certainly knows where to get it. My door is always open for her!" Rhodan said firmly.

The flight to Venus was uneventful. It took not more than three hours, since the average speed of the *Good Hope* was about thirty-five million miles per hour.

The three American astronauts were totally overwhelmed

by the miracles of Arkonide technology that permitted such undreamed of flight performance. Even Nyssen was overcome by the superiority of the aliens' scientific achievements. Freyt felt so small and insignificant opposite such limitless superiority that he began to ask himself how Rhodan had reacted to that shock when he had had to face it.

The yellow globe of Sol's second planet soon appeared on the *Good Hope*'s screens. First a fuzzy picture that soon gave way to the cloud shrouded image of the planet Venus. The yellow globe soon filled the whole video screen, and soon only a partial view of the planet was visible. The astronauts were able to discern the stormy activity of the Venusian atmosphere.

The Venusian day is ten times longer than an Earth day, since Venus completes one revolution around its axis in two hundred and forty hours. Also the distance from the sun to its second planet is thirty percent less than that from the sun to its third satellite. These two facts cause a tremendous difference in temperature of the diurnal and nocturnal zones, despite the planet's protective atmosphere. This difference in day and night temperatures gives rise to terrible wind storms, against which our own Caribbean hurricanes seem like a mild breeze.

The *Good Hope*, however, was not affected by these atmospheric disturbances. Although she offered a good target for the three hundred mile per hour winds, once she had dipped down into the Venusian atmosphere, the spaceship's stabilizing energies were strong enough to keep her on an unimpeded course.

A few months earlier when Rhodan had first visited Venus, he had made a cartographic outline of the Venusian topography. He had arbitrarily selected some point through which he drew the lines of the artificial network covering the whole surface of Venus.

Rhodan planned to establish their base on the equatorial continent that stretched from sixteen degrees south to twenty-two degrees north, while its longitudinal borders ran from zero degrees to fifty-four degrees west. Its surface was equal that of South America. Its easternmost point Rhodan had named Cape Canine, since its outline closely resembled the head of a dog. The longitudinal line that touched the outermost tip of the dog's pointed nose had become zero degree of Venusian longitude.

Rhodan had so far left unnamed the continent itself, as well as the oceans that surrounded it. However, he had carefully studied the continent's topography and had decided to establish his base on the north coast near where a six mile wide river entered the ocean. The land was covered with dense jungle forests that reached up to the top of the highest mountains. It would not have been advisable to go further inland with their future base.

Since urgent affairs on Earth had not permitted Rhodan's first expedition to stay sufficiently long on Venus, they had been unable to explore its plant and animal life thoroughly. All they had been able to find out in their limited time had led them to believe that this continent was inhabited by gigantic prehistoric life forms, not unlike the fauna and flora of Earth in its youth.

The planet's favorable atmosphere had been the determining factor for having chosen Venus as the base where they could withdraw in case of danger on Earth and where they would also be able to carry on without interference the additional training the mutant corps needed. The atmosphere was sufficiently dense to lessen the heat from the sun to a point where the temperature was bearable for human life. The average midday temperatures on the equatorial continent ranged in the nineties, while the nights hovered around forty-five degrees. The everpresent cloud cover did not let any bright sunlight through, thus bathing the Venusian surface in a gloomy glow.

"Cape Canine!" announced Bell, who was sitting at the direction finders.

Rhodan was flying the *Good Hope* with manual control now, ready at any moment to rectify its course should any mistakes crop up in the cartographic picture he had so hurriedly compiled during his first expedition. He dared not trust the automatic control with such delicate maneuvers.

Rhodan compared the image on the video screen with his map of Venus. The river delta where he intended to land was still more than two thousand miles away.

"The Thousand Bend River!" Bell called out.

That was the name they had given to the wide river that

117

wended its way down to the ocean in numberless serpentine loops.

From now on Bell made regular announcements, accompanied by descriptive remarks. He had an excellent memory for anything pertaining to maps and landscapes.

Freyt, Nyssen, and Derringhouse remained silent. They were awe stricken. Khrest and Thora sat next to each other on a couch, busily observing the picture screen. Tako Kakuta and Anne Sloane had come into the command center, watching the scenery of the strange planet below, whose surface kept steadily coming nearer. Rhodan waved a friendly hello to Anne, who had hardly left her cabin since they had started from Earth.

Manoli was busy with his radio installation. He kept glancing at the picture screen. He seemed disgusted that there was no radio signal coming from Venus he could intercept. In case there should be any intelligent life on the planet below, they certainly had not yet evolved any wireless communication system.

"And down here," Bell continued, "is the—"

That was as far as he got. The craft received a sudden violent shock that jolted it off-course, toward the south.

The alarm sirens began to howl.

We are being attacked! thought Rhodan, who reacted with the speed of lightning.

"Thora! Firing position!"

By her quick reaction Thora proved that she could, if necessary, overcome the inertia of her race. "Ready to open fire!" she shouted.

"Have you located anything yet on the direction finder, Bell?"

"Nothing so far."

"Use the outboard instruments! Try to find out where the disturbance came from!"

Rhodan quickly turned to Thora. "Be sure to wait until I give the order to open fire!"

She simply nodded.

Rhodan applied optimum thrust. The *Good Hope* pushed with all her might against the strange force that had thrown her off-course. Rhodan glanced at the direction finder screen the same instant Bell reported, "Directional gravitational field, coming from three degrees east of due north!"

Rhodan had expected that much. Any lesser force could have been easily overcome by the *Good Hope*.

"Give me the exact location where the gravitational force beam is originating."

While Bell was feverishly making his calculations, Rhodan stated with grim satisfaction that his craft was managing to keep its position, by using a full counterthrust against the pull of the beam.

"Point of origin of the gravitational field beam, twenty-nine degrees eighteen minutes north, fifteen degrees forty-eight minutes east."

"Thora?"

"Ready!"

"*Fire!*"

Thora pushed down on a switch that released an instantaneous swarm of six gravitational rockets, which could be seen on the picture screen at once as bright streaks, streaming toward their target.

These gravitational torpedoes were capable of causing tremendous damage upon impact. Depending on the stability of the target they would either seriously damage it or tear it apart, by releasing a gravitational shock wave. Because of the five dimensional character of the gravitational energy, any protective shields that were applied against their force would have to be immensely complicated structures. Thora hoped that their opponent, whoever he might be, did not possess such energy barriers.

Thora's rockets rushed toward their destination. They attained speeds of Mach ten. It was just a question of a couple of minutes until the enemy would be hit and then cease to exist.

Suddenly the unbelievable happened. Rhodan had been busy regulating the thrust of his nuclear engines, while Bell was occupied with the direction finder, trying to locate the enemy positions precisely. Thora was therefore the first to notice the amazing chain of events. The whole rocket formation, which so far had moved north in parallel trajectories, changed course abruptly and turned east. The formation soon disappeared over the rim of the observation screen.

Thora was thunderstruck, unable to call out right away.

When she finally alerted Rhodan, it was too late for him to see where the rockets had disappeared to.

He rushed back to his pilot's console to supply thrust with which the *Good Hope* could neutralize the still effective gravitational pull coming from the enemy camp in the north.

Who could be strong enough to withstand an attack with Arkonide weapons? Rhodan wondered. The Mind Snatchers —the M.S.! This was Rhodan's first thought. But quickly he rejected this possibility, for the unknown enemy had not tried to destroy them, the way the M.S. would have done. The pull of the directional field of gravity was a mild force compared to the punishment such a powerful opponent could mete out, an opponent who had pushed aside the six Arkonide rockets as a man would shoo away that many flies with a wave of his hands.

Despite the flood of thoughts that filled his mind, Rhodan kept busy steering the *Good Hope* down toward the ground, all the time pushing against the enemy's pulling beam. He expected another more effective and more dangerous attack from the enemy at any moment, but nothing happened. He tried to imagine the mentality of the opponent who was evidently concerned with seizing the *Good Hope*, which came as an invader in its territory; but this was an enemy who, on the other hand, did nothing when the invading ship evaded its gravitational pull.

In the meantime, under the influence of the pulling beam, the *Good Hope* had reached the fortieth parallel of the planet's northern hemisphere. They had passed the coastline of the northern continent whose southern border roughly followed the outline of the thirty-eighth parallel.

"We are going to land here!" Rhodan informed his crew. "I hope to escape the unknown force beam. It will probably be easier for us to approach the enemy's positions on the ground. We have no other choice. The enemy is stronger than we are, at least as concerns the amount of energy he has at his disposal. Let's hope that he has not achieved a higher level of technological development than our Arkonide friends. I do not think that our unknown opponent can locate us once we have landed, for we can hide our ship in the jungle that seems to cover the northern hemisphere. As long as we move in or slightly above the jungle we will remain invisible to the enemy from his position far to the north. But since we can't simply ignore the presence of the unknown enemy, we have no alternative but to approach his positions by creeping through this jungle."

Reg was just about to express his opinion, when another unforeseen event took place—Dr. Manoli's receiver suddenly intercepted a radio communication!

Manoli's receiver worked on the principle of hyperwaves; accordingly, the enemy's sender must be of the same type, which meant that they had reached a very high level of technological development.

From the receiver emanated a series of distinct acoustical entities that resembled words but that no one, even Khrest, could understand.

Rhodan instructed Manoli, "Answer them! Tell them we have come with peaceful intentions! But we protest any undue interference with our spaceship's course!"

The doctor carried out Rhodan's orders. But he had hardly finished his transmission, when a new message came in. Like the previous one, this was totally incomprehensible for all aboard the *Good Hope*.

Rhodan asked Manoli to move aside so that he himself could broadcast in the Arkonide language, which was the *lingua franca* of the universe. But the enemy's reply was again a mystery to them. It seemed as if they were constantly repeating the same phrases, over and over again.

"Khrest!" Rhodan called to his friend, who all this time had been sitting quietly on his couch. "I am going to take out the tape. Will you feed it into the automatic translator and see what it can make of this unknown language."

Rhodan cut off the piece of tape from the recorder that automatically recorded any communication, and handed it to Khrest, who would have the message analyzed and translated by the translating machine. In the meantime the messages from the unknown sender had ceased. Rhodan was uneasy, for this might mean renewed attacks from the enemy. There was the possibility that the enemy used the gravitational beam as a rather unusual method of orientation, some kind of a lighthouse beacon that guided the enemy's own returning ships. Perhaps he had realized by now that their messages had not been answered in the expected manner, that some hostile strangers were approaching!

Rhodan tried to set the *Good Hope* down as fast as

possible. The altitude diminished rapidly, and when they had descended to a height of a thousand feet they had escaped the influence of the opponent's gravitational pull entirely. Once again the craft was under Rhodan's control, and he could maneuver it whichever way was necessary.

Bell had returned to his post to continue with his observations of the terrain below them. They had penetrated the thick cloud cover that had obscured their view, and now at an altitude of three miles their optical picture screens began to function. They could clearly see the hilly and sometimes even mountainous landscape of the polar continent.

"Mountain ranges up to eighteen hundred feet above sea level," announced Bell.

Rhodan was pleased. "That will do for us. We can easily hide there our one hundred eighty foot high spaceship."

Bell began to compare the picture showing on the detection finder with those appearing on the optical screen. The *Good Hope* kept descending.

"Look, over there! That's our spot for landing!"

Rhodan saw a gently ascending chain of hills that stretched in a northeasterly direction. About two-thirds up the mountainside yawned a craterlike depression. It was circular and about six hundred feet across at the rim. It was not possible to judge the crater's depth from the spaceship's present position.

Rhodan maneuvered the *Good Hope* to a point three hundred feet directly above the middle of the crater, from where they had an excellent view of the whole structure. It extended to a depth of almost two hundred forty feet, with gently sloping walls, unlike the steep walls characteristic of volcanic craters. Rhodan noted this last point with some relief.

"Okay, I am setting her down now! This looks safe enough!"

The crater floor was overgrown with a dense thicket of low bushes and occasional trees. Carefully Rhodan lowered the huge spaceship down into the crater. Soon the turquoise colored stop signal lit up on the control panel. The *Good Hope* had come to rest in its nest, where it was safely hidden from the enemy's view.

CHAPTER THREE

Khrest had completed his task at the robot translator. He stepped over to Rhodan to hand him the paper strip with the transcribed message. "The translator identified it as an archaic form of Rim Galacto," reported Khrest. "Here is the translation."

Rhodan took the paper strip and read the Arkonide syllabic script. "Transmit the code signal, as agreed!"

Bell peered over Rhodan's shoulder. He was just as fluent in the Arkonide language as Rhodan, Thora, or Khrest.

"As agreed?" he repeated. "Who agreed what with whom?"

"Let that be our last worry, Reg!" said Rhodan. "I am much more puzzled by what he means by 'Archaic Rim Galacto.' "

He searched his memory bank for the information he had obtained during his hypno training sessions. Rim Galacto? Archaic Rim Galacto?

Khrest, too, was at a loss. Rhodan knew of the existence of Rim Galacto. It was a dialect of the official language spoken throughout the Arkonide. This dialect was limited to the far outlying areas at the rim of the galactic empire. This special version had developed during the past millennium. The attribute "archaic" seemed to indicate that there existed a still more ancient form of that language. But neither Rhodan nor Khrest could tell when and where and by whom it had been spoken once upon a time.

In any case the dialect was so old that any resemblance to modern Galacto had disappeared.

"This doesn't tell us what we need to know," said Rhodan. "We will have to go right to the source where this message came from and find out on the spot."

This transcription convinced Rhodan more than ever that the unknown foe could not possibly be the greatly feared Mind Snatchers, who might have constructed a secret hiding place on Venus. For the M.S. were known not to need a spoken or written language for communicating with each other. This thought was some comfort to Rhodan, even if he had no assurance that the strangers were not far more dangerous than the M.S.

He let his gaze wander around the cabin, resting for an instant on each member of his crew. "No sense wasting any time. Before the day is over, our scouting party must be well on their way to the enemy's lair."

"How do you evaluate the situation?"

Rhodan and the two Arkonides were sitting together in Rhodan's cabin. Reginald Bell, Tako Kakuta, and the three American astronauts had left the *Good Hope* half an hour earlier in order to make a cartographic survey of the area.

"No evaluation is possible," countered Khrest, "as long as we lack any hints of who opposes us here."

"Did you consult the archives?"

"Yes, but without result. The archives contain no information about this planet. It is not on the list of inhabitable planets we encountered on our galactic expeditions."

"This confirms my own thoughts," remarked Rhodan. "For if anything were recorded in the Arkonide archives I should have learned of it during my recent hypno schooling. I should have remembered for sure if I had learned anything in the first place of archaic Rim Galacto. Worse still, I don't have the faintest idea how this lingo might have come about."

Khrest remained silent for a while, preoccupied with his thoughts. Then he spoke up. "A possible explanation might be that in the very first stages of our galactic explorations, an Arkonide expedition reached these outposts and then shortly thereafter cut off communication with our home planet. They might have done so deliberately or they might have been overwhelmed by some catastrophe. This could perhaps explain the fact that our archives lack any data about this colony."

"That would mean that this colony must be at least fifteen thousand years old according to terrestrial time," Rhodan said.

"Correct. This is the date when our first efforts at colonization began. A few hundred years later our communications system had been perfected to such a degree that any newly established colony could never have been forgotten."

"Well, let's assume these people are Arkonides like you

and Thora, but Arkonides who left their home planet fifteen thousand years ago and lost contact with the civilization of their race. They must have evolved a different life style in the meantime. You don't even speak the same language any more!"

"What do you mean, Perry?"

"Regardless of whether we are dealing here with members of your own race, Khrest, we must consider them our foes. And they will remain to be so until we have informed them of our intentions. As soon as they have learned why we have come here, our unknown opponent will decide if they are for or against us."

"Or they might remain neutral!"

"Neutral? Do you really believe anybody will be able to remain neutral in this sector of the universe in view of the events that seem inevitable in the near future?"

Rhodan fell silent for a few moments. Then he resumed the conversation. "We will have to stalk the opponent, cautiously approach his base as if he truly were our enemy. Otherwise they might detect us and wipe us out.

"As soon as we have reached their base we must attack. We will try to cause as little damage as possible. But we are forced to attack if we want to get near enough to them to have a personal confrontation. I am convinced they won't welcome us at the gates and invite us in! Therefore, what's the use of debating any longer now who the opponents are, how they got here?"

Khrest pondered awhile. "The dynamics of your logic frighten me, my friend. Although my mind has many more years of training than yours, it would have taken me several hours to arrive at the same conclusion. However, there still exists the chance that we might have to shoot at our own kind."

Rhodan rose. He was about to answer, when Thora interjected, "Has it occurred to you that these colonizers have inhabited this planet for many thousands of years without leaving any apparent trace of their presence?"

"Yes, I have been puzzled by this. Even the smallest group of settlers would have to leave their imprint on the surface of this world. But what have we seen? Nothing but jungle, water, and volcanoes. Not the slightest trace of any civilization."

"Except for the small matter of a directional gravitational field and the apparently effortless manner with which our six combat rockets were deflected from their course!" Khrest remarked, not without a trace of unaccustomed sarcasm.

"All right, their base might be a marvel of technological accomplishment. But there is nothing else outside that base!"

"What conclusion do you draw from that?" asked Khrest.

"None so far. We will have to wait until we get inside their base. Only experience can tell."

At 180 hours local time Bell and his group returned to the *Good Hope*. They brought back a relief map that the automatic cartographer had produced during their survey of the surrounding countryside.

Bell proudly presented the map to his friend Rhodan. "We have completely covered an area with a sixty mile diameter around the spaceship. It was no child's play, even with the Arkonide transport suits we were wearing. We hardly dared climb more than one hundred fifty feet above the treetops."

"I wonder if you didn't go up too high," Rhodan said, with worry in his voice.

"Too high—one hundred fifty feet? The enemy base is at least three hundred miles from here. How could they possibly . . ."

"The Arkonide transport suit uses artificial gravity. Such a force can be detected over a distance of thousands of miles."

Bell was startled. "You are absolutely right. Why didn't I think of it! But let me tell you what else we found. That might calm your fears."

Bell pointed to the map. "This area has direct access to the ocean. Not even six miles from here we have found a fjord that is still six hundred feet wide at this point."

"A fjord?"

"Yes. The water is salty but has no waves. Maybe it is a salt lake."

"Go on."

"The water is teeming with life. There are all kinds of fish and a seal-like creature. The rest of the animals are horrible to look at and unlike anything we have on Earth. A huge octopus that could hide a whole squadron behind its body; sea serpents with six feet; and something that lies on the surface of the water like a colorful carpet. Not until you touch it does it spring to life. Of course, we didn't do anything as foolish as that, but we threw a stone at the thing. Suddenly the beautiful carpet changed into a broad grayish clump that enveloped the stone and dragged it down into the deep water, where it disappeared."

Rhodan laughed. "What else have you found besides these monsters that seem to have come straight out of a horror movie? Anything important to report?"

Bell was crestfallen. He had thoroughly enjoyed his own gory story. "The terrain is sloping toward north, rising gently but steadily. Far to the north we sighted a mountain range, with peaks up to thirty thousand feet. The interior of this continent is a vast array of mighty mountains, but the highest are in the area where the enemy has his base. We also noticed several ugly looking volcanoes.

"The landscape is rather uninteresting in all other directions. It remains at the same level in an easterly and western direction, only rarely dotted by a few hills. Toward south the land slopes down to the ocean. The air smells most unpleasantly of fire and sulphur, but it is breathable, without making you feel nauseated. And there are animals as tall as the Empire State Building."

Rhodan snickered skeptically. "Come off it, Reg!"

"They are *huge*, Perry! But they don't appear to be smart. Nyssen tested their reaction time. He'd hover directly in front of their big mouths and could easily get away before they'd even see him.

"There are also two little rivers that run southward. That's all we found. We marked anything worthwhile on this map."

Rhodan nodded, pleased with what he heard from Bell. But then he insisted, "You wanted to explain why the unknown foe can't locate you, even if you were flying one hundred fifty feet above the treetops."

"They are sitting right in the middle of the mountains. Considering the large number of high elevations, the probability seems very great that their view will be obstructed by at least one of these high peaks."

Rhodan inspected his friend from head to toe. "It hasn't occurred to you that they would have placed their observation posts on the highest mountaintop, stupid?"

"Well . . . but . . ," stammered a very embarrassed Bell.

"You bet your sweet bippy they saw you cavorting around," said Rhodan. "And may God have mercy on you if you gave away our position!"

For a few moments Bell was a pitiful sight. But then he rallied from his depression. "I think they'd have started shooting at us long since if they had sighted us. I am sure they did not see us!"

Rhodan simply shrugged his shoulders. "Who knows? Maybe you were lucky!"

Shortly after 190 hours dusk fell, accompanied by heavy storms. (Rhodan had outfitted the most important chronometers on board the *Good Hope* with dials adjusted to Venus's daily rotation on its axis. A day had two hundred forty Venusian hours. Each Venusian hour was fifteen seconds shorter than one hour on Earth.)

Rhodan had decided to keep the scouting party on board the *Good Hope* a while longer and to continue exploring their immediate vicinity. He wanted to find out which instruments and tools would be most suitable if they had to make their way through the Venusian jungle. But in addition, he preferred waiting until he was sure that Bell's reckless behavior had not alerted the enemy as to their presence. If indeed they had become aware of the Earthlings, the humans would no longer be able to use their Arkonide transport suits—at least not for flights above treetop level. Below on the jungle floor the suits were worthless anyhow. The dense jungle of the polar continent made any attempt at flight impossible.

Rhodan set up a continuous guard system. At least one man who was familiar with the search instruments and safety installations of the *Good Hope* had to stay in the command center at all times. In case of emergency it was not sufficient that they could come running from all parts of the ship on hearing the alarm signal.

Rhodan ordered each guard to record on tape any observations or incidents, regardless of whether they had any bearing on the specific tasks of this expedition. Any observation, including natural phenomena or animal behavior, assumed importance when it supplied additional information to the scouting party regarding the world around them.

Rhodan himself had the first guard duty, from 191 hours till 193 hours. He extinguished the light in the central command room. He was all alone. He raised an optical probe as far as the rim of the crater in order to get a thorough look at the surroundings.

The storm outside raged with unbelievable fury, coming from the east. With the help of an aerodynamic probe Rhodan measured the wind velocity, which close to the ground was two hundred and ten miles per hour, far less than it had been at higher altitudes.

Dusk had given way to total darkness at about 192 hours. Rhodan had to switch the optical probe over to infrared frequencies. This caused the pictures on the receiver screen no longer to appear in their true colors. Instead, everything was visible as white on a black background.

Half an hour later the storm had spent itself. On the picture screen Rhodan perceived the long, snakelike neck of a saurian type creature, rising above the leafy roof of the dense jungle. The tiny head swung at the end of the neck like a pendulum. Perhaps the animal was trying to find its bearings after the storm. Rhodan observed how long the creature needed to accomplish its task. Bell had been right—these animals were not well endowed with intelligence.

Rhodan flipped on the tape recorder to register his observations. "Dinosaurlike creature. Head about five to six yards above the roof of the jungle. Takes about ten minutes to orient itself, although environment is unobstructed."

That was a valuable bit of information. Such observations would save time when the scouting party encountered such a beast. No necessity to make a wide detour around it! They could probably crawl right between the creature's legs, and it would not notice them.

Suddenly Rhodan was startled by a noise coming from behind him. He whirled around, to see Thora enter the room, which was only faintly illuminated by the glow of the picture screen.

"You sure startled me, Thora!" Rhodan laughed nervously.

"I have come to relieve you, Perry. It's almost time for my turn at guard duty."

Rhodan glanced at his watch. He still had another twenty minutes to go. In silence both stood and watched the bright screen.

"You should have seen this area when the storm was raging," he remarked after a while. "It looked quite romantic."

She did not reply. A few minutes later she posed the strange question, "Do you like it?"

"What?"

"This world."

"I like any new world that I have a chance to see. I have been informed about most of them—quite thoroughly in many cases but only sketchily about several of these worlds. But I will not feel totally satisfied until I have been able to see all of them wih my own eyes."

Rhodan remained silent for a few moments before he added; "Why do you ask? Don't you like this world?"

She hesitated slightly, then said, "I don't know whether you can understand me. Being a member of my race makes me realize that there is really nothing new anywhere in this universe for us to see. Whatever we discover in one place we have already seen elsewhere in a similar or even identical form. You get tired of discovering these old 'new things.' Do you follow me, Perry? I wonder how long before one of our philosophers will get around to demanding that we abolish spaceflight, since it no longer contributes anything to the further intellectual development of our race."

Rhodan pondered this. It did not seem absurd to him at all, considering the history of the Arkonides, who for many thousands of years had been busy exploring other worlds. Not too surprising if they could no longer find anything new.

"But your spaceships have never ventured to other galaxies. Or at least none of their attempts have been successful. Might such new adventures not infuse your tired people with a new zest for life?"

"You are talking like an Earthling," she answered, with a hint of sarcasm in her voice. "Young, curious, and a bit violent. Just think how much such an intergalactic expedition costs and compare that cost with the returns."

"Who has ever worried about the costs of a new, world shaking cause?" Rhodan said with irritation. "The development of Earth's space technology, until they finally built the moon rocket, was extremely expensive. All mankind could have lived in luxury if they had spent the money on themselves rather than for space research. But did such considerations prevent our progress in space flight? No! People in Asia, Africa, and Latin America kept dying by the millions from starvation or from diseases that could have been cured if there had been enough money for food and medication. Instead, we constructed the moon rocket! I wonder about the ethics of behavior that permits millions to die for the sake of progress. In any case, men seem to be a bunch of hardheaded creatures more concerned with satisfying their curiosity and exploring the unknown than with regaining the idyllic conditions of a Garden of Eden for all mankind.

"But who knows what humanity's fate would have been had we acted differently? Maybe we would no longer exist! We have gone through so many catastrophes that came close to extinguishing us."

Rhodan had spoken with vehemence, but Thora understood that he did not mean to attack her. It was his pride in mankind that had caused him to flare up. Suddenly she felt a surge of envy rising in her. "I don't know if we ever, even at the height of our existence, were so full of energy!"

Rhodan turned around and tried to peer into her face as best as darkness would permit. Her reddish eyes were glowing in the weak reflection of the bright picture screen. It did not appear that she was making fun of him and his kind. Her attitude of resignation caused him to worry and made him feel helpless.

He looked at his watch. It was time for him to go off duty. "I enjoyed talking with you," he said stiffly. "I hope we will find more opportunities for such dialogues in the future."

She did not reply but simply smiled at him as he turned to leave. As soon as he had closed the door behind him he felt sorry that he had not stayed longer with her. She had come earlier than necessary to relieve him. He could have remained awhile to keep her company. She was probably disappointed now. He was almost about to open the cabin door again but then changed his mind. What if she looked at him in her usual sarcastic manner? No! This would completely spoil the good feeling their conversation had aroused in him.

Slowly he walked back to his own quarters. He sat down and smoked a cigarette, lost in pleasant thoughts. Then he switched on his video screen, but since his set lacked an outside probe, all he could see were the dark walls of the crater that hid the *Good Hope*.

Rhodan did not know how long he had been asleep when he was awakened by the hum of the telecom.

Bell's round face appeared on the screen. "Wake up, Perry!" he shouted. "Wake up!"

Still half asleep, Rhodan fumbled for the telecom switch. "What's the matter?" he grumbled.

"I've seen something interesting here that—"

"Why don't you record it on tape and let me sleep!"

"No, Perry!" yelled Bell. "You got to listen to me! The seals have climbed ashore and up the mountainside, where they have gathered for a meeting. *That* you must see!"

"The seals? What seals are you talking about? Since when do seals conduct meetings?"

But then Rhodan remembered Bell's report from the previous day. Suddenly he was wide awake. "Give me two minutes and I'll join you."

Rhodan found Bell sitting open mouthed in front of the video screen. Bell motioned excitedly to Rhodan but did not say a word, as if he were afraid to scare the animals away by his voice.

Rhodan noticed that his friend was using the optical probe together with a sectional enlarger. Thus he had managed to bring the small plateau of the mountaintop so close that they were able to recognize the smallest details, although it was almost five miles away. The mountain was about fifteen hundred feet high. It was totally overgrown with low bushes, except for the plateau at the top.

Rhodan checked the time. It was a few minutes before 196 hours. Soon Bell's turn on guard duty would end.

Then Rhodan concentrated his attention on the video screen. There were a number of strangely formed animals moving around on the plateau. They faintly resembled seals, but according to Bell's previous description they breathed through gills.

Rhodan was fascinated by their strange mode of loco-motion. Something caused them to jump simultaneously, all in the same manner.

"What do you make of it?" asked Bell.

"You said they are true fish, Reg. And here they are jumping around on dry land!"

"Odd, isn't it? But they do have gills, and as long as we observed them they never surfaced from the ocean."

Rhodan thought a moment. "They could be some kind of lungfish that can survive for some time out of their element."

"I'm not so interested in how these creatures breathe, Perry. I'd much rather know what they're doing over there."

"Well, let's find out directly," suggested Rhodan. "Get us two transport suits!"

Bell jumped up, full of excitement. "I thought you'd never get around to suggesting that!"

Rhodan went to the telecom and called Khrest, who was due for guard duty after Bell's turn. Rhodan informed the Arkonide scientist about Bell's observations of the herd of seals and that they intended to stalk them. They wanted to get a close look at them and, if possible, capture one of the seals.

Khrest quickly agreed to relieve Bell early.

As Rhodan and Bell were leaving the *Good Hope*, dressed in their Arkonide transport suits, Reg remarked, "How come you're no longer worried that the enemy might detect us if we fly over to that mountaintop?"

As Rhodan carefully shut the outer air lock, he explained, "To begin with, I don't intend to fly one hundred fifty feet above the treetops, as you did. And furthermore, that summit over there affords us excellent protection."

In slow flight, they glided close along the crest of the hills. Rhodan had equipped himself with a needle ray gun, while Bell was carrying a somewhat heavier disintegration instrument.

The night was quite dark. The difference between the distinct picture they had seen on their observation screen and the impenetrable blackness around them now was at first quite irritating. But even under the cloud cover of the planet Venus, there were occasional isolated flicks of light, and little by little the two men's eyes became adjusted to that inadequate illumination.

It took them barely fifteen minutes to cover the five miles to the mountaintop. They had purposely moved rather slowly, so as not to alert the seals to their coming.

They observed the creatures for a few minutes. The seals were about a yard long. Most of the time they moved about like true seals, simultaneously on their tail and side fins. But occasionally during their dance they managed to balance themselves only on their tailfins for almost thirty seconds at a time. They made a very funny impression on the two men, who could not imagine that these creatures could ever become dangerous to anyone, even if they were attacked.

Then their antics abruptly came to an end. Rhodan became aware of how silent the herd of seals seemed to be. The only sound they made was the shuffling of their flippers on the bare ground.

Now they were evidently getting ready to depart, probably to return to the waters of the ocean below. Rhodan nudged Bell, giving him the signal to get ready for action. They rose from behind the low bushes where they had taken cover, and with a couple of wide jumps they reached the herd.

The creatures reacted instantaneously. Most of the group darted off in frightened leaps over the far side of the plateau and down a steep slope. Others tried to reach the protecting ground cover to the other side of the plateau. Only one seal had not moved fast enough to escape the quick grasp of both Rhodan and Bell.

Oddly enough, the animal did not struggle when it realized that it had been captured. It lay motionless on its back, peering at the two men with wide open, intelligent eyes.

"Watch out!" warned Rhodan. "This might be a trick. At the first chance he'll make a dash for safety."

But the little fellow did not appear to have anything of the sort in mind. He remained docile and let himself be picked up by the two men, who quickly flew back to the ship.

In the meantime Khrest had alerted the rest of the crew that something interesting was taking place. When Rhodan and Bell carried their prisoner into the central command room they were welcomed by the waiting crew.

"What do you intend to do with that creature?" inquired Dr. Manoli.

"I would like to have your advice on that, Doctor," answered Rhodan. "These seals seem to be of a relatively high order of intelligence, but how can we find out for sure?"

"Why not try a cerebral analysis?" Bell interjected.

"That presupposes that the creature is capable of forming logical thoughts," countered Rhodan. "But it is worth a try."

The seal was resting on a lab table. Dr. Manoli examined the animal with deft and gentle manipulations. "Too strange," he murmured after awhile. "I am absolutely convinced that the animal is capable of emitting sounds. I wonder why it remains so silent."

On a small instrument table that had just been wheeled into the command center, to be placed next to the seal's head, was a small, thin walled glass container. Suddenly the container began to vibrate and emitted a high humming sound. Finally it jerked sideways and then shattered into many pieces. Dr. Manoli stared at the glass splinters with a perplexed expression.

"Of course," said Rhodan. "I should have thought of that before! Let's get the ultrahigh frequency sound receiver!"

From the lab was brought equipment designed to establish communication with aliens. This special apparatus transformed ultrahigh sound frequencies into the normal hearing range.

The instrument was placed next to the little seal. At once a series of humming, squealing, and twittering sounds could be heard. These were recorded on tape, which was fed into the cerebral analyzer, together with the encephalogram of the creature's brain waves. On the basis of these data the analyzer could correlate sound with meaning and eventually reconstruct the language of the creature. This was, of course, possible only if the sounds represented a true language, and not simply a series of inarticulate utterings of fear, excitement, or anger.

The analyzer amplified the brainwaves and gave them meaning on the basis of a kind of thought pattern installed in its memory banks. This procedure was based on the principle that the same thought emanating from different brains would emit identical impulses as long as the brain belonged to the C-O-H group, typical for organisms living in an oxygen atmosphere.

The instrument produced the result of its analysis in the form of special cards that in turn had to be deciphered by the computer. The whole procedure took barely two minutes.

Rhodan took the plastic card that the computer had spewed out and read out the message printed in Arkonide characters. "I, your most humble (not decipherable, probably a name), beg the exalted (meaning gods or deities), to permit me to return to my element (the ocean?), to prevent my imminent death from asphyxiation."

Rhodan finished, then stood for a moment totally perplexed. Then he quickly rallied and called Tako Kakuta, the teleporter.

"Tako! Quick! The creature is suffocating. You must return it at once to the water so that it can breathe again. Can you carry it back to the ocean?"

Tako smiled and took the seal into his arms. "Sure. Will do. It isn't heavy. I'll be right back."

Only a few seconds had passed before Tako made his reappearance.

Everyone in the command center fired questions at Rhodan, which he tried to answer as best he could.

"We are undoubtedly dealing here with an intelligent life form. We have proof in the fact that the analyzer was capable of deciphering its thoughts. But on the other hand, these creatures must be some kind of lungfish, with a dual respiratory system. They obtain oxygen either from water through their gills or from the air through their lungs. But apparently the latter method is not yet fully developed in these creatures and permits them to stay outside the water for only a limited time. That's all."

Rhodan fell silent, pondering further the implications of their encounter with the seal type animals. After some time he added, "We will, of course, try again to establish communication with them. We will learn their language first and then talk with them. But let me make this clear to you —these seals are definitely not the same people that have established a base far to the north of here. The seals could not be capable of such tremendously advanced technological feats."

CHAPTER FOUR

Originally Rhodan had planned to let the scouting party start only after sunrise. But the Venusian night proved to be too long for the impatient human complement of a crew that was hungering for action.

Therefore Rhodan had the members of the scouting party equipped with Arkonide transport suits, as well as weapons and rations to last them several months, well ahead of schedule.

The troop consisted of Rhodan, his friend Reginald Bell, Dr. Manoli, the three American astronauts, Tako Kakuta, and finally Anne Sloane, who had insisted in participating in the scouting mission.

Rhodan had just completed briefing his group, which was now ready to pass through the air lock, when suddenly Khrest's voice was heard over the ship's telecom system: "Stop! Wait! Sightings!"

Rhodan asked his group to wait and rushed back to the command center, where he found Khrest sitting in front of a radar scope, on which a swarm of white light dots darted aimlessly back and forth.

"What is that, Khrest?"

"I am inclined to believe that these are robot spies. I don't know whether you remember that we had similar structures in the early stages of our history. They are simply either radio, optical, or microwave probes with a considerable range. These instruments here on the screens are most likely no larger than my head."

"Judging by their aimless movements they have not yet located us," stated Rhodan.

Khrest shrugged. "Don't be too sure. This may just be one of their tricks."

Rhodan thought for awhile; then he decided. "We will leave as planned, despite these robot spies. But we will proceed on foot rather than fly. We will take along a robot to clear the way through the jungle."

Rhodan glanced at Thora. He wanted to find out if she was afraid. But she just smiled at him.

"I'll keep in constant touch with you," said Rhodan. "Don't take any risks with the safety of the *Good Hope*. If you should think that our protective force fields can no longer shield you from enemy attacks, you should lift off and make a getaway.

"We will do our utmost to defeat our opponent, whoever he might be. But in case we fail, we will arrange for a meeting place where you can pick us up, or . . ." He hesitated briefly. "There might be none of us left for you to pick up. That's a chance we have to take."

Khrest looked serious. He was once again impressed by the Earthling's audacity. Thora had stopped smiling.

Rhodan rushed off to rejoin his scouting party, which was waiting for him at the air lock. Rhodan instructed Bell to fetch a heavy robot ground leveler from the ship's storeroom. This robot would have to do its work in a semiautomatic fashion, since there was not enough time left to program it for full automation. That would mean that someone would have to guide the robot during his work performance.

"We will keep on our suits," Rhodan declared after Bell had left on his errand. "But I will wring your necks if you fly above the treetops without my express permission!"

Bell steered his robot out through the air lock. The others followed one by one. They reached the upper rim of the crater at thirty minutes after 239 hours, which was just half an hour before the Venusian midnight.

Rhodan let his group march down the other side of the mountain toward the fjord.

The discuslike robot spies had disappeared from the radarscope, as Khrest informed them via radio.

The descent on foot turned out to be quite difficult. Fortunately, though, the mountain slope was free of any plant cover. Evidently nothing had been able to take root on the steep incline because of the fury of the frequent storms. At the head of their small procession the robot rumbled along. It had no ground leveling work to perform here, since there was no plant cover. The bulky robot had a hard time maintaining its foothold. It was followed by Rhodan, who led the rest of the scouting party. Tako Kakuta formed the rear guard.

The descent toward the ocean took more than an hour.

A new Venusian day had begun in the meantime, but it was still as pitch dark as before.

During that time they had covered only a little more than a mile, as the crow flies, from the crater rim to the edge of the sea. Rhodan calculated that it would take them two hundred fifty hours if they continued toward the enemy's stronghold on foot. True, the descent had been especially difficult, but on the other side of the fjord they would not encounter any more favorable conditions, since the gently rising land was covered with dense vegetation.

Rhodan decided to fly across the fjord, utilizing their Arkonide transport suits. The rising slope on the opposite side of the fjord made them undetectable as long as they flew close above the water.

The robot crossed the fjord in its own way. Splashing wildly it stomped down into the water, and soon the waves closed above its metal head. It was of such sturdy construction that it would be safe from any dangers that might lurk in the waters of the fjord.

The robot's impetuous advance caused quite a ruckus among the inhabitants of the waters. Rhodan noticed thin shapes flitting ahead of it through the air, probably some kind of flying fish. From the side there came the mourning cries of a creature that had never been beheld by any human eye. At some spots in the water the glow of colored lights suddenly appeared.

"These are the carpets," explained Bell. "The robot seems to have stimulated their appetites, and now they are trying to lure their prey."

The scouting party still stood on the shore. No need to hurry, since flying across would be much faster than the robot's slow progress through the water.

Anne Sloane pushed her way close to Rhodan. "It's pretty scary here, don't you agree?" she asked, as if Rhodan were a teenage pal of hers.

Rhodan gave a signal to his troop. "Let's go!"

The first to disappear, naturally was, Tako Kakuta.

"Oh, to be a teleporter!" sighed Anne Sloane enviously.

Their flight proceeded with barely a sound, in contrast to the noisy protests of the citizens of the ocean who protested against the intruders. As Rhodan flew over one of the glowing carpets, the carpet seemed to rise toward him, then contracted, glowed more intensely, and finally condensed into a faintly shimmering ball that sank swiftly below the surface of the water. The creature must have realized that it had missed its aim and beaten a hasty retreat.

The crossing lasted less than two minutes. By constant shouts, Tako guided them to a place that was free of any vegetation. This would be a good bridgehead on which to gather their forces before their advance into the jungle. This spot was slightly off their course; consequently Bell activated the guiding beam that would let the robot emerge from the water at the desired place.

Fifteen minutes later the robot waded ashore. They hardly recognized it.

"Lights!" ordered Rhodan. "Get the robot cleaned up!"

An impenetrable tangle of vines completely covered its hull. Bell made the robot stop and had Anne direct the beam of her manual searchlight on the confusion. Bell resolutely attacked the tangle, trying to pull it off the robot. He seized the plants with both hands.

Suddenly he cried out and pulled his right arm out of the tangle. Startled, he looked at the strange, oddly shaped creature that had sunk its teeth into his glove and now dangled from his hand. The animal resembled a rhesus monkey. Its eyes were covered with a keratinous film that must protect them against the salty sea water, but made them look lifeless, like white marbles. Instead of a hairy fur the animal had a covering of sleek scales. Its tail ended in a pair of short pointed prongs. Since the creature was violently thrashing about, especially with its tail, Bell ran the risk of injury despite his resistant transport suit.

"Throw the thing away!" shouted Rhodan.

"That's easier said than done!" snarled Bell. "I can't pry it loose from my glove."

Bell tried to get hold of the tail and pull at it, but the monkey reacted by increasing the intensity of its bite. Its teeth sank even deeper into the thick leather of Bell's glove. Bell let go of the tail, but the monkey was now violently whipping him with the released tail, whose prongs managed to rip Bell's suit.

All Bell's frantic maneuvers remained without success until he hit on the idea of beating the monkey over its head with his clenched fist. One strong blow caused the animal to lose consciousness and finally to loosen its grip on his glove. Like a stone it plummeted to the ground.

Bell picked up the motionless form and inspected it closely. Anne came wandering over to him.

"He isn't dead," Bell assured the girl. "Just unconscious. You see? He's coming to!"

Hissing like a cat the monkey snapped at Bell's hand again. But he reacted in time and flung the creature back into the water.

This experience caused Bell to proceed with greater caution while he cleaned the tangled plants from the robot.

At long last the job was completed. Bell shone the light into every crack to make sure nothing was hidden inside the robot's structure. Then he slapped the robot's domelike top playfully. "Next time I'd better carry you piggyback! Look at all the trouble you caused me!"

Rhodan had a short final conversation with Khrest; then he gave the signal to start. The fight against the jungle had begun.

The robot—they had named it Tom in the meantime—exceeded their expectations. It flattened and rolled aside the underbrush like straw. At the same time it produced such a racket that all the bizarre looking creatures that might have alarmed the men behind Tom now fled deeper into the forest in panic. Prudently, it circumnavigated the larger trees. It was not only powerful, but it also possessed the ability to distinguish clearly between those obstacles it could assail and those it could not.

They were only a half hour underway before a stop had to be made because Bell's hand began to hurt him. Anne examined it and determined that the water monkey had bitten through his glove. After being treated with an application of Arkonide medicine, it was only a few minutes before Bell was relieved of the pain.

"I hope that this will serve as a warning to all of you," said Rhodan. "We should get used to a simple rule—don't touch anything! As long as everything in this world is strange to us, consider all unknown gadgets and whatnots as too hot to handle."

Then, protected by Tom's broad stern, they continued onward. The small lane that he carved out for them was wide enough for two men abreast, with an overhead clearance of about eight feet. Rhodan watched carefully above them, searching the foliage overhead with the spotlight, not certain what animals might be living there, but nothing was discovered.

After a three hour trek they made a halt and set up a temporary camp. The men paired off, and for each group of two they erected one of the Arkonide inflatable tents that, when deflated and pack folded, could fit in the average pants pocket. Anne was the only one with a private shelter.

The continuing darkness produced some uneasiness and confusion among the men. They stretched out to catch a few winks of sleep, but only a couple of hours passed before they were on their feet again. Rhodan had stood watch. He did not feel tired, and he took the opportunity to communicate with Thora. Through her he learned that the small robot spies had made a second appearance but that they had retreated with as little success as on the first occasion. No other enemy activity had been observed.

Nothing of an unusual nature occurred during the two hour rest period. Rhodan was glad—they could do without any unpleasant incidents. As for his personal instinct for adventure, he was a bit disillusioned. A few minutes before the end of his watch, when he heard the rhythmic rumble of some saurian creature's passage in the vicinity, he considered it a poor substitute for a noteworthy experience.

They established thirty hour time periods, and during two of them they advanced about fifty miles. This was a remarkable accomplishment, considering that they were traversing impenetrable jungles and were burdened with the presence of a woman.

There were no untoward events.

Toward the end of the second thirty hour period, after Tom had quickly created a clearing for them and they had put up their tents, a new day appeared to be dawning above the forest canopy. Rhodan sent Tako into the treetops to determine how close they might be to their objective.

After a few minutes, Tako came back and reported, "Less than a hundred miles to the north, the real mountains begin. Even in the poor light and at this distance you can't mistake those towering walls of rock. It's going to be a rough job to climb up there."

Meanwhile, with help from Derringhouse, Bell had fixed something to eat. They all ate somewhat wearily and then crept into their tents. Captain Nyssen had the first watch, but it passed uneventfully. The Venusian jungle creatures seemed to fear the alien intruders.

Several hours later, calamity struck in full measure.

Dr. Manoli had the watch. He sat in front of his tent, which he shared with Tako, and against Rhodan's instructions he had turned off the spotlight, to make it easier for him to observe his surroundings. The jungle's leafy canopy was no longer able to screen out the gathering brightness of the new day, which began to dispel even the deeper ground shadows around him. It was the seventy-first hour, by log time—actually the start of the second day of their Venus sojourn, if one were to reckon by Venusian days.

He had become accustomed to the normally clamorous sounds of the jungle; but suddenly Manoli heard something that seemed to come from the immediate vicinity of the camp itself. Hurriedly, he put the light on again and listened.

Hearing a distinct scraping noise, he stood up and tried to determine where it was coming from. He panned the beam of the searchlight around the camp but could not uncover anything that looked suspicious.

Then he heard a piercing scream, so terrifying that he felt the goose flesh jump across his back. It was Anne's voice, and with three or four rapid bounds Manoli was at her tent. He ripped the entrance flap aside and shone his lamp into the interior.

Anne was not to be seen, but the thing that threshed about in her place was so horrifying and repulsive that he was momentarily frozen in his tracks. The thing had neither an end nor a beginning. As thick as a human thigh, it was a coiling mass of slime coated pale white flesh that had crawled up out of the ground. Except for a slightly perceptible series of circular depressions, the creature showed no evidence of an articulated structure or any sign of limbs. Manoli was certain that it had bored the hole out of which it now emerged. The other extremity of the thing was already beyond Anne's tent. The body continued to ooze up.

143

out of the hole, to gather in a sickening mass on the other side of the tent. This was the scraping noise that he had heard.

Suddenly Rhodan was standing beside him; the scream had brought him out of his tent in a hurry. "What is it?"

Manoli did not need to explain. Speechlessly and with a trembling gesture he pointed at the pale white monstrosity. Rhodan appeared to grasp the situation instantly. He turned his head. "Bell! The disintegrator!"

A shouted answer was heard from outside. Rhodan lifted his needle ray gun, aimed it at the quivering white mass, and pressed the trigger. He did not take his finger off the trigger until a smoking, odorous incision had been cut straight through the creature's body. The result was astounding. The forward end appeared not to be concerned with what had happened to the rear portion. It crawled away and in a few moments had completely disappeared from the tent.

Meanwhile, the second portion, with the singed front section, undulated uncertainly back and forth on the edge of the hole. Then it suddenly began to change. With a soft crackling sound, the burned crust fell off the end, and the exposed cross-section extended itself out into a headlike tip. Then the remnant animal set itself in motion again— out of the hole, through the tent, and away.

This exhibition had lasted only a few seconds, during which time Rhodan realized that this was no way to help Anne. He plunged out of the tent and yelled for Bell.

"Here!" came his answer.

"Some kind of giant worm has grabbed Anne and taken her off," explained Rhodan rapidly. "Apparently it's as hard to kill as an earthworm. We've got to run it down!"

Together, they ran around Anne's tent and discovered the second worm segment crawling away in the slimy trail of the first segment. Bell drew in his breath sharply between his teeth at the sight of it; then he raised the disintegrator and started to carve out a tunnel in the jungle along the worm's path. He knew what had to be done—they had to get past the second segment and overtake the first one. There or somewhere in between they would discover Anne.

Rhodan had considered that he might send Tako ahead

of them, but the goal was uncertain and the danger too great.

With a desperate fervor the two men rushed into the breech that had been made in the foliage, carved it out deeper ahead of them, stumbled over vines and creepers, fell several times with a moist slap against the body of the second worm, struggled against nausea, and got up again to run onward.

Rhodan was aware that they were not advancing very rapidly. With each passing minute they gained only about a yard on the worm, and from what he had seen so far, its stretched out length exceeded all expectations. Merely to reach the front end of the second worm segment took ten minutes. Bell turned around and permitted the destroying beam of the disintegrator to play over the scarlike body until it had dissolved into nothingness.

"Be more cautious with the other one," admonished Rhodan. "I don't know if worms have the ability to sense that they are in danger. If this one has, it might disappear into the ground with Anne."

Bell nodded. Simultaneously he used the disintegrator to lengthen the jungle passage, through which they now pressed further into the forest. Rhodan beamed his flashlight ahead and discovered the tail end of the first worm disappearing into the brush at the end of the leafy tunnel.

They plunged in behind it. While they were busy overtaking the tail of the creature and pressing through the side branches beside it where Bell's short range disintegrator shots hadn't reached, they failed to notice in their excitement that the ground was starting a gradual upward incline. Even if they had noticed it they would not have attributed much importance to it.

This first worm segment was even longer than the one they had destroyed. It took them almost a half hour to gain sight of the blind pointed head of the creature—which also brought Anne into view. The worm had thrown a coil about her body, and with its forward section rising sharply upward, it held its victim up high. Apparently, Anne was unconscious. She hung limply in the coil of worm flesh, but it seemed that nothing more serious had happened to her so far.

While they were catching up with the worm and figuring

out a way to free Anne from her terrifying predicament, they failed to notice that the jungle was opening up into a clearing only sparsely covered with underbrush.

"I'll go as close underneath her as possible," Rhodan said finally. "When you fire at the thing I'll be able to catch her."

Bell nodded, completely depleted of words. He waited until Rhodan had established a favorable walking position alongside the continuously crawling worm; then he began to fan the white body with the uninterrupted beam of the disintegrator. Where he aimed, the worm dissolved into vapor. The thing seemed to become aware that it was in danger, and it turned to one side. Bell had to jump away to avoid having his legs sideswiped.

The creature stubbornly continued to move until Bell had disintegrated about seven-eighths of the body mass that he could see from where he stood. Then the movements and twitchings suddenly died. Its forward part toppled, but Anne was still clutched in the coil. For fear of hitting her, Bell did not dare to shoot at this part of the animal.

Rhodan executed two slices with his needle ray, which cut the rest of the worm into three parts; then he withdrew the girl from the clammy, cloying embrace of the coil. Carefully, he set her body on the ground in an area that appeared to be safe, and then he tried to bring her back to consciousness.

Neither of the men noted that a few yards ahead the ground opened up into a circular hole of considerable radius and depth. Neither one saw the bizarre, multiple limbed creature that shoved itself over the rim of the hole like a thin, glistening tree limb with many side branches and approached them with jerky movements.

Rhodan studied the trail of slime the worm had left on the ground. The body of the animal must have measured more than forty yards in length, he reflected. Considering that the beast had not completely emerged from its hole before he and Bell took off in pursuit of its forward segment, what must its total length have been? Everything on Venus seemed to have been created too large—the worms, the lizards, the flying fish. Only where the process of evolution reached a certain state of intelligence did the giantism cease. The seals had proved that point, and perhaps also the little water monkey that had bitten Bell's hand.

On the other hand, this giant worm had been relatively defenseless. Its only weapon seemed to be its repulsiveness. It had been able to throw a coil around Anne and carry her away, but not once had it made an attempt to defend itself against their attack.

Anne opened her eyes. She looked about her, at first confused, then with a sudden look of fear in her eyes. With a half articulated cry, she recognized Rhodan and grasped his arm.

"Where are we? What happened?"

Gently but firmly, Rhodan forced her to lie back on the ground. "Don't get excited—it's all over now," he said.

"What was that—" She put her hands over her face as memory returned. "Something grabbed me and took me away. It was so clammy and hideous! What was it?"

"A worm," replied Bell. "A plain old garden variety of earthworm—or should I say Venusian worm."

She regained her composure slowly. After a while she removed her hands from her face to look at Rhodan. "Where is it? Did you . . . ?"

Rhodan nodded. "Bell wiped it out. How do you feel?"

"All right, thank you—except for the scare. How for are we from camp?"

"About an hour away. When you feel better, we'll start back."

This was agreeable to her. As she sat up, her glance happened to pass beyond Bell's squatting figure—and then she saw it.

"*No!*" she cried out, and as she sprang up she fell into Rhodan's arms.

"What's the matter?"

"Look there!"

In a phlegmatic calm, Bell remained sitting on his heels, looking up at her. Only when she pointed close behind him did he make a move to turn.

"Don't move!" bellowed Rhodan.

Bell froze.

Rhodan saw the cause of Anne's excitement. It looked like a long, thin branch with numerous smaller twigs. But one would not expect such a branch to lift up its twiglike arms, as it did now, and poke at Bell's suit. The entire creature must have been about six feet long and, raised up on its spidery twig legs, about three hands high.

Rhodan drew his weapon and carefully cut the animal into two parts with a single shot. The twiglike legs buckled and with a weird rustling sound the creature collapsed to the ground.

Rhodan holstered his ray gun. "Okay—now you can get up," he told Bell.

Bell jumped up and turned around. "What was it?"

"That thing there—the branch."

Bell bent over and was about to pick it up.

"Keep your cotton-picking fingers off of that thing!" Rhodan bellowed. "Man, don't you ever learn!"

While they were concentrating their attention on the dead animal in an attempt to learn what sort of life form it was, Anne looked about the area. She discovered the second twig legger and screamed.

Rhodan took long enough to observe that the thing was crawling directly out of the hole; then he shot again with his ray gun. Apparently these branch creatures were far more articulated in their structure than the worms. One shot, however, and the thing was killed on the spot.

Bell had now become alerted. He raised the barrel of his disintegrator and moved furtively to the place where the second creature had apparently come out of the ground.

"Careful!" Rhodan called to him.

Bell annihilated a patch of scrubby undergrowth and stood on the edge of the hole, which had escaped their attention until now. Rhodan heard him cry out in astonishment and quickly joined him. Speechless with a sort of shocked revulsion, Bell pointed downward into the pitlike orifice, which the dim light of dawn penetrated only weakly.

Rhodan turned the beam of his lamp into the hole, which was about nine feet wide. Its depth was difficult to calculate because a rustling, scrabbling mass of twig leggers nearly filled it. There must have been hundreds of them, and they seemed to be expecting something. Bell raised the disintegrator, but Rhodan held his arm.

"Look!" he said.

In addition to a busy confusion that seemed normal to the twig leggers, something else was stirring them up. The sea of wriggling limbs seemed to swell; then something white appeared in the blur of spidery legs and branchlike bodies and emerged—the tip ended head of a worm such as they had just destroyed.

It pursued its course resolutely, jerkily raising its thin head higher and higher out of the rustling confusion of the twig leggers, apparently intent upon reaching the very edge of the hole, where Bell and Rhodan were standing.

"All right," Rhodan ordered. "Fire!" The head of the worm weaved back and forth within a handbreadth of his feet.

Bell obliterated the worm and the entire contents of the hole with the ravaging beam of the disintegrator. It took him a minute, perhaps slightly longer, and then the pit was completely empty. They could now see that the whole excavation was about five or six yards deep. At its bottom yawned two other dark holes of about the thickness of a man's thigh—ingress and egress for the worms, which appeared to have lived together with the twig leggers in a strange symbiosis.

Anne shuddered and clung to Rhodan's arm.

"Let's head back," he ordered. "In the future we'll know just how careful we have to be."

Rhodan hung a portion of the first twig legger over the barrel of his ray gun and brought it back to the camp with him. Although the creature appeared to be dead, he didn't dare to touch it with his hands.

At the campsite, Manoli and the others had overcome the rest of the worms that had crawled out of the hole. Rhodan gave the twig legger fragment to Manoli.

"Examine it as best you can," he said, "but avoid touching it."

Then he gave them all a briefing on what they had experienced during Anne's rescue.

When Dr. Manoli completed his examination of what Rhodan had brought him, he explained, "The creature is composed almost entirely of a horny substance. It has a minimum of organs, and even they are of keratinous construction wherever the organic function is not involved."

He paused for a moment, poking through the dirt on the ground with a stick. "I've been cudgeling my brain over some things we've found here, and I've made a test of the slimy substance that was left behind by the worm. The stuff contains such a terrific complexity of proteins that it's impossible that they could be manufactured solely by the worm itself.

"My theory is this—in contrast to our own variety of earthworms, this Venusian worm creature is a typical carnivore or more precisely, it feeds on the *insides* of animal life forms. On the other hand, the twig leggers live off of that portion of their animal prey which contains any horny substances. Moreover, they are not themselves capable of catching such food. Opposed to this, the predator worm apparently has no teeth or chewing equipment with which to pierce the outer skin or shell of captured prey, and the outer covering is inedible to the worm anyway.

"So these two types of organisms have made a sort of biological covenant between them. The worm captures the prey; the twig leggers tear off the skin or shell and devour it. Then, more or less as a payment for services rendered, the worm gets to eat the innards. This is the strangest symbiosis I have ever come across."

Rhodan caught Bell staring very fixedly at Anne, who was puzzled by his rather pale faced expression. Bell finally shook his head and said, "I'm glad we got there in time—about thirty seconds to spare, I should say."

CHAPTER FIVE

On the rest of the trip toward the enemy base there were only two events of significance.

The first involved a call from the *Good Hope*. Khrest and Thora reported that the enemy had not been heard from but that the seal creatures had put in another appearance. In a forced march—apparently to reach the water in time—they had crossed over the mountain and climbed down into the crater.

"Do you know what they have done?" asked Khrest, amused.

"No."

"They've deposited a great pile of fish by one of the launch tubes—apparently as an offering to the gods!"

Fortunately, Thora had observed their approach and had installed the thought analyzer in the tube. The analyzer had picked up the seal creatures' thoughts, and using data gathered by the ultrasound detector, the autotranslator was now able to reconstruct the larger part of the seal language. Khrest had removed the fish, in order not to disillusion the seals should they return. On the next occasion he was hopeful of being able to talk to them.

The second event involved an encounter with a Venusian saurian monster, which they had so long anticipated—but this was not so amusing. . . .

Of the total distance of three hundred miles, by this time they had put about two hundred forty miles behind them. They had already traversed two mountain chains and had discovered behind the second one a long, narrow valley whose floor was covered with a thick jungle.

Rhodan felt tempted to permit the use of the transport suits so that his group could fly over the fairly deep valley. But he finally decided that the sixty miles still separating the scouting party from the enemy did not offer a safe distance for their operation. With proper instruments, gravity waves were one of the most easily detected manifestations of energy. Within a certain proximity from the scanner site, even the laws of geometrical optics no longer applied. At close range a sensitive detector could recognize a source of gravitic energy even around corners.

Consequently they clambered down into the valley and prepared to slice their way through the jungle behind Tom's broad back. Anne Sloane was the first to sense that something was wrong ahead of them. She stopped suddenly so that Bell, who was walking behind her, bumped into her. Rhodan noted that something was going on behind him, and he also stopped. Only Tom flailed his way unerringly forward until Bell shouted a command that brought him to a halt.

"Didn't you hear anything?" asked Anne, puzzled.

Bell shook his head. "No—nothing. Did you?"

Anne nodded energetically. She was about to speak, but a loud rumbling sound interrupted. The ground trembled at the same time, and this time everybody noticed it.

Rhodan recalled the rumbling he had heard at the first camp. "A dinosaur!"

151

"What's it doing?" asked Bell. "What's making all that thunder?"

"It's walking!"

Bell listened. After a protracted moment, the rumbling was heard again. He laughed. "Walking, eh? With a half minute between his steps?"

Rhodan nodded gravely. "It could happen—if the thing is as big as I think it is." He beckoned to Tako. "Tako, go aloft and see if you can make him out."

Tako disappeared. A few seconds later he was back. "He is coming from the east," he reported. "If he keeps his present course he'll bypass us about two hundred yards to the north."

"Then go back upstairs and watch to see that he doesn't change his direction."

They waited. There was no point in continuing onward just now because they were headed north and would probably succeed only in getting under the dinosaur's feet. As the moments passed the rumbling increased to the intensity of a small earthquake. Rhodan tried to peer through the leaves in the hope of at least seeing the giant creature's neck, but the jungle thicket that was capable of offering protection against Venusian hurricanes was also capable of cutting off his view.

The next monster tread occurred with such force that even Rhodan was shaken. In the next instant, Tako was beside him.

"He's changed his direction—coming right on top of us!"

"How far away?"

"Another two steps and he'll be here!"

Everybody heard this. Rhodan looked at them. "No time to get out of the way, but we can defend ourselves!"

Bell got the picture. He fetched the expedition's two disintegrators on the double, gave one to Rhodan, and made ready with the other.

"Aim straight up!" Rhodan ordered. "If he falls, let's make sure his body disintegrates before he hits the ground!"

Bell nodded agreement.

Rhodan turned his head to shout over his shoulder. "Remain close together!"

From the distance a loud roaring was heard as if from a waterfall. The colossal dinosaur was shoving the jungle aside with his tremendous body. Then, suddenly, it became dark. A deep shadow appeared to fall upon the forest, and a few seconds later, not five yards away from Rhodan, a monolithic, granite gray pillar of flesh thundered into the thicket with an ear shattering blast of sound. Rhodan noted the scaly, dirty skin, then turned his attention upward to the thing that moved above him. He perceived the situation at a glance and shouted in alarm.

"Look out! He's passing right over us!"

This the creature actually did. At the next interval of his stride the other pillarlike leg crashed down through the jungle on the other side of them to Bell's left, and simultaneously the mighty animal jerkily dragged its low hanging body completely over the trembling group of tiny humans.

During this experience it seemed as if a complete darkness was upon the world. Four or five yards above them the foul smelling belly of the dinosaur was suspended, but the stink was the least of their worries. The question was, would the hind legs pass them by as harmlessly as the front ones?

Rhodan lowered his disintegrator. "Look out for the tail!" he shouted to Bell. "He can wipe us out with a single blow!"

Barrroom!—the first hind leg. The gargantuan body mass shoved itself forward by a mighty stride, and the light of day was seen from the north. Bell closed his eyes and turned his head, waiting.

Barrroom!—the second hind leg.

"Thank God!" groaned Bell; but then he opened his eyes to watch for the tail.

Rhodan stared upward and attempted to figure out where the animal's tail would contact the ground. He was still calculating, when something colossal swept close over his head, followed by a wail of wind.

"He's turning to the right!" yelled Bell.

Rhodan cocked his head to the side and saw the shadow of the several yards thick tail swish to the east. In the same moment the titanic animal took its next stride. Rhodan swung the barrel of the disintegrator and waited. If it required a thirty second interval between the creature's steps, how long would it take for the tail to pass?

Nothing else happened. The great, columnar legs of the

dinoasur thundered away at the same rhythmic pace, but the feared disaster from the tail did not occur. It seemed to Rhodan that the animal had again swerved from its course and that it was now walking in the direction in which it had originally been moving. This would explain why they failed to see any more of the tail.

A few more minutes passed in tense, alert readiness; then tight arms and shoulders relaxed, and they began to believe that the danger was behind them.

Bell relinquished his grip on the disintegrator and wiped the sweat from his forehead. He was able to grin again. "Footprints seven yards apart," he said. "Any shorter than that and we'd have been clobbered!"

They arrived at the conclusion that the dinosaur, including body and tail, must have been over six hundred feet long. According to Tako's information, Rhodan judged its height, including the long neck and head, to be over two hundred feet. Even by Venusian standards it must have been a monster; but in any case it far outclassed any saurian life form that had ever existed on Earth.

Toward noon of the third Venusian day since leaving the *Good Hope*, they arrived in the region they suspected of harboring the enemy base. This terrain was a complete contrast to what they had seen during the first two-thirds of their march. They were at an altitude of about eighteen thousand feet above sea level, and although the Venusian atmospheric density was appreciably higher than Earth's their breathing began to be difficult. The ringing in their ears due to high atmospheric pressure, which they had experienced in the lowlands, was now replaced by a ringing in their ears due to low atmospheric pressure.

They had left the jungle behind them, having passed the timberline at about sixteen thousand feet, and the mountain locked plateau where they now stood exhibited very little flora—pale, sparse grass, stunted bushes, and a few gnarled and twisted trees that hunched along the ground instead of lifting their branches to the sky.

The last stretch upward to the plateau had unnerved them. Many times they would have given up, but when it no longer helped to think of the enemy that they must ferret out and subdue, then Rhodan was always there at his self-appointed task, driving them with his will alone. They had reached the southern rim of the plateau in the early glow of dawn. They had then pressed northward along the western extremity of the lofty plain, always under cover of projecting cliffs or traveling in rocky recesses or declivities, and now they found themselves at the northern wall of the lofty enclosure.

Mountains towered above them, more tremendous than any they had seen thus far. Rhodan was convinced that the enemy would have established his equipment on the highest pinnacle in order to have as wide an effective range as possible. But even with the best of telescopes Rhodan could see nothing from his position below the mountaintop. If there were any installations up there they were either built into the cliffs or excellently camouflaged. Here, then, at the northern extremity of the plateau, Rhodan ordered a campsite set up to serve as the springboard for all further operations.

On the afternoon of this day they investigated the environs of the camp in two separate groups. Tako Kakuta with Captain Nyssen and Lieutenant Colonel Freyt even climbed more than three thousand feet higher into the mountains, but the only thing they found was a dead animal that looked like a fox.

Only Anne Sloane and Lieutenant Derringhouse had remained behind in the camp. Anne serviced the small scanner detector device, which compensated for its inferior evaluation in the eyes of the Arkonides by being sensitive to multiple forms of energy. It could locate electromagnetic transmitters as well as gravitational wave sources, but in the first few hours of its operation at the new campsite it did not pick up a thing.

The enemy was silent.

Rhodan continued to feel uneasy. As long as he didn't know where the enemy sat, it was quite possible that their new camp lay before him on a silver platter. While they strained their eyes in search of these hostile beings, the latter were probably sitting somewhere among their lofty crags permitting themselves to be amused by the futile temerity of these bumpkin invaders, before becoming bored and deciding to attack. It was a small consolation to him that every consideration had been given to all conceivable dangers and directions of attack; the main fact was that none of this was a guarantee against the possibility that there was a chink somewhere in their armor, through which the enemy could see.

In the second thirty hour period after the camp had been established, they launched the search in earnest.

This time Tako and the two Americans took the direction in which Bell, Rhodan, and Manoli had searched the last time, and the latter three climbed up the mountain in Tako's previous tracks. The first part of the climb over the first comparatively mild slopes of the forty thousand foot peak was made comfortably and without encountering unusual difficulties—but also without making any discoveries. They detoured around a wide, rock strewn slope and finally climbed up a steep incline of the wall behind it. The spot where Tako had turned about on the previous day was still two hundred yards above them.

It took them an hour to conquer this particular stretch. The place where Tako had found the fox creature yielded nothing new, and there were no signs of any visitation since. They were about to turn back, but before they started to climb down Rhodan cast his glance once more above him and suddenly tensed.

"Hey! Look at that!"

Everybody stared upward, and it was some time before they discerned what he was pointing at. The upper part of the mountain wall seemed to lie back a bit more to the north than the lower part. An actual break was nowhere to be seen, and the homogeneous gray granite of the escarpment offered no contrast for them to estimate the setback distance between the two surfaces. But in any case there seemed to be some sort of a plateau up there that had been invisible to them until now.

Rhodan continued climbing. The escarpment began to be more challenging. Utilizing a sort of rock chimney formation as a channel for footholds and body bracing, they managed to shove themselves another hundred yards or so toward their goal; however, the remaining hundred and fifty feet that now separated them from the clearly distinguishable precipice edge seemed to be insurmountable.

It was an accident of circumstance that came to their

aid, and they could thank a certain intermittent occurrence for the fact that they were not made the victims of a powerful mechanical action but moments before. As lead man in the file of climbers, Rhodan was the first to sense a vibration in the rock wall above the chimney. Something of a threatening nature seemed to be approaching from an undetermined direction, and he braced himself firmly and drew the needle ray gun with his free right hand.

Suddenly he heard a hollow sound like the blast of a mighty exhaust through a tube, and as he turned his head he saw close behind him that the air was shimmering under vibration and dust swirled out from between two boulders. The phenomenon was at first unexplainable. The air seemed to be hotter than its surroundings and was being emitted under terrific pressure through the opening between the rocks. Moreover, Rhodan now noted that an arrangement of flatter rocks above the chimney they had just traversed was apparently acting as a deflection shield, driving the exhausted hot air down the chimney.

Observing the two outlet boulders, he could see with what powerful force the hot air was propelled down the chimney. Had they still been down in that channel, they could not have survived such an infernal hurricane.

The phenomenon lasted for about two minutes. Then the exhaust roar became weaker, the shimmering of the air lessened, and finally the noise died entirely. Under the clouded sky the gray wall of the precipice loomed as peacefully in the diffused light as it had before.

During those two minutes, no one had spoken a word. But now Rhodan pointed to the two boulders and shouted, "Maybe we can find a better way over there—come on. And hang on tight if that blast comes again!"

With Rhodan this time bringing up the rear, they all fingered and toed their way across. Bell was the first to arrive at the opening between the boulders. For a moment he peered inside suspiciously; then he took a step forward and disappeared. Manoli followed him, and then Rhodan. They discovered that the two boulders were nothing more than the outlet of an exhaust tunnel of about five foot width that led upward at a comparatively gentle angle. The walls of the tube were strangely smooth, so that the upward climb was difficult in spite of the reasonable grade.

Rhodan egged them on anxiously, admonishing them to hurry. He was certain that the smoothness of the tube was a result of the hot air blasts such as they had just witnessed. Apparently they came at regular intervals or at least frequently within certain time periods, thus enabling the heated air streams to leave the same fluid dynamic traces as might a constant stream of water.

Gradually the steepness of the channel lessened. Apparently the upper end of the tube ended on the plateau. However, this hope was not completely fulfilled. It ended in front of a low frontal wall that exhibited a ragged dark hole in its middle, but the wall itself was only about seven feet high. With a hefty swing, Rhodan hoisted himself over it.

Here was a sort of platform, an open area of some one hundred thousand square feet extent, enclosed at the back by a horse shoe shaped cliff wall. At first glance, the unusual smoothness of the rock floor irritated Rhodan's eyes, but at second glance he discovered in the steep back wall a row of dark openings set fairly close to the floor of the platform. He knelt down and examined the ground. The others had joined him by now. Noting nothing unusual other than the smoothness of the rock floor, he stood up and nodded toward the openings in the wall.

"Let's take a look at those," he said.

A strange uneasiness came over them as they moved gingerly toward the wall. The holes were ragged and jagged. The men held their weapons on open safeties, ready to fire, because there was something suspicious about the brooding calm of the place. At close range and in spite of their jagged outward appearance, the openings turned out to be fairly circular in shape, with a diameter of about three and a half feet. Their center points were at about the height of a man above the platform floor. The distance between the holes averaged about twenty-five feet.

Rhodan stopped within a few steps of the wall and lifted his hand. Bell stood to his left, Manoli at the right. Rhodan strained to penetrate the darkness of the hole in front of him, but without success.

Bell, who stood in front of a second opening, said in a low voice, "I can see something!"

Rhodan joined him, and when he peered into the second

aperture he began to make out a gray, shadowy outline. He couldn't quite determine what it was. He motioned for Bell and Manoli to stay where they were; then he moved further forward. He approached the opening to within three yards, never removing his gaze from the gray shadow they had discovered. It took the shape of a cylinder that extended out of the darkness to the edge of the hole.

When he recognized what it was, panic struck him for a moment. Never in his life had he seen a disintegrator of this tremendous size nor one that pointed so precisely at his gut. With a wild leap, he jumped forward, and as he fell to the ground he yelled at Bell and Manoli.

"Hit the deck!"

A few minutes prior to this, inside the mountain, the following developments had occurred.

The robotic scanner and coordinate locator had made an observation and reported to Command Central: "Three entities are entering the landing plateau through the exhaust tube. They are . . ."

An exact description followed—or more precisely, this was the accompanying text for a video strip the scanner locator station had started transmitting to Command Central from the moment Rhodan had appeared over the edge of the plateau from the tube.

In the Command Central, as it developed, there seemed to be some dissatisfaction with this report. A request was made for special details concerning the kind of clothing the strangers were wearing. The automated observation post proceeded with a special structural scanning analysis and submitted the results.

A short time later it received the order "Continue scanning! Standard report mode!" And it busied itself complying.

Meanwhile the commanding entity had set other communications in operation and advised the Sector F fire control station, "Alert standby, condition three! Program for controlled fire. Shoot only on order from the commander!"

For the commander had determined from the scanner data that with such entities as the three who had appeared, it wasn't just a matter of indiscriminate firing. Moreover, this whole matter was perplexing. It cost the commander a strenuous mental effort to arrive at the conclusion that nothing definite could be concluded from the mere advent of the strangers or from their mere appearance or type of clothing. After all the years the commander had spent in this fortress, peacefully and undisturbed, he experienced a kind of impatience with the realization that he had to wait a while longer before his curiosity, or what passed for curiosity, could be satisfied.

So it was that everything remained quiet for the moment. The commander observed the electro optical report of the scanning station and waited. . . .

After Rhodan had lain on his belly for five minutes without anything happening, he began to chide himself over his original alarm. Whoever had installed these disintegrators had undoubtedly made the installation at the same time that the rock floor of the plateau had been glazed. Rhodan had no idea how long it would take the process of normal weathering to reduce the floor glaze to chips and blemishes, but certainly it would have to take at least a thousand years. It was improbable that the disintegrator muzzles, which were equally exposed, should have been able to withstand the weathering action better than the floor glazing.

He had rolled against the cliff wall in his dive for cover. In getting to his feet he held himself to one side and slowly slid along to the mouth of the aperture. Inch by inch he brought his head to the edge of the hole and finally looked inside. The muzzle of the disintegrator was so close to him that he could have reached out and touched it with his hand. It had a diameter of slightly under two feet. Between its barrel and the wall of the aperture there was enough room to slip through.

Without taking too long to weigh the risks, Rhodan swung up and hunched into the opening. For a breathless moment he poised with his entire body exposed to the awful muzzle; then he forced himself into the hole next to the barrel. He slid along the astonishingly smooth metallic plastic and almost fell to the uneven floor of a cave for which the aperture more or less served as a window.

He waited for any possible reaction, but none came. Then he stepped to the window hole and called to Bell and Manoli, telling them to follow him. As a precaution he motioned them not to come directly in front of the disintegrator.

Rhodan's reckless entrance into the cave was by no means overlooked by the commander. The uninterrupted report coming in from the robot scanner detector plunged him into a new perplexity. It was difficult to imagine that anyone of this stranger's appearance and type of clothing would be foolhardy enough to climb right over the muzzle of a disintegrator.

The commander was forced to admit that the actions of this intruder did not coincide with his expectations. But he still lacked important information, without which he was not in a position to reach a final decision regarding the three strangers. . . .

They were not equipped for searching a cave, since they had not brought along a flashlight. The dim light of day that came through the gun ports penetrated the inner gloom for only a few yards. Behind the second and fifth apertures stood disintegrators. The other four ports seemed to serve no other purpose than to admit light.

Rhodan examined the disintegrator that he had climbed over. It was constructed on the same principle as that of the smaller installation on board the *Good Hope*, but Rhodan knew that this was no definite clue to the racial origin of its builders.

Meanwhile, Manoli and Bell inspected the walls of the cave and took a look at the second disintegrator.

At the first disintegrator, Rhodan noticed that it had no operating controls. Moreover, he was amazed to see that the weapon was a fixed installation that could fire in only one direction. Of course, this disadvantage was compensated for by the fact that the neutralizing crystal field would be fan shaped at any desired spread angle. Two disintegrators of this type, spaced as they were here, would easily have the range and coverage to sweep the plateau clean of any opponent.

Nevertheless, Rhodan was gravely disturbed by the absence of any control mechanisms. The box at the back end of the heavy weapon he found to contain merely the generator for powering the crystal field.

Manoli and Bell joined him.

"Well, isn't that a letdown for you?" said Bell.

"What do you mean?"

"This cave. We expected a gigantic fortress, and what do we find? A lousy hole in the mountain!"

Rhodan smiled. "Have you located the gravitation generator?"

"What?" Then it came to Bell, and he slapped a hand to his forehead. "Say, that's right! Where is the generator?"

Rhodan continued to smile. "The people who made this cave were probably counting on your kind of reaction," he said. "The cave is so constructed that it would lead one to believe that there is nothing else here, unless that person possessed our own level of experience and training. If in addition the intruder knew nothing about disintegrators he would probably be disappointed and leave. Now then— here's something else. . . ."

He revealed to them the absence of operating controls. "The conclusion is that the disintegrator is remote controlled—but from where? Certainly not from some corner of this cave. And I'll show you something else." He passed his hand over the mirror smooth surface of the disintegrator barrel. "Granted, metallic plastic is a durable material—it can last a century without corroding. But if we consider that these disintegrators have probably been here as long as that glazed platform outside it will give some idea of what these barrels would look like by now, if it weren't for the fact that they have been carefully maintained and polished."

Bell had already got the impact of this, but Manoli's mouth gaped open in surprise.

"Then you mean that there must be people around here who come in regularly to maintain these weapons and polish their barrels?" he said.

"Something like that."

"But where are they?"

Rhodan shrugged. "I'm not clairvoyant. But besides all that, there is still a more important question. Since these disintegrators are so well preserved, they can obviously be put to use. But nobody fired at us. If we can assume that the beings who have built this stronghold utilize human logic, then it might be expected that they could desist from hostilities and perhaps seek to communicate with us. So— where are they?"

The Commander waited. . . .

"There's no going on from here," Rhodan decided after they had spent an hour inspecting the cave walls without success. "We'll have to get Tako and Anne Sloane up here. Anne could try to locate an exit mechanism and find a way to operate it, if there is one here within her range of perception. If that doesn't work, we'll simply have to send Tako into the mountain."

Manoli wore a dubious expression. "In other words, a kamikaze mission."

Rhodan shook his head. "Don't be silly. Tako's teleportation faculty obeys physical laws. He can never rematerialize inside alien matter—he has a sort of emergency brake for such cases. If there is no hollow space inside the mountain, he will automatically return to the place he took off from."

"What I had in mind was his solo confrontation of the enemy," Manoli corrected himself.

"They haven't done anything to us—why should they do anything to him?"

Manoli shrugged.

Bell had another suggestion. "Why don't we try using our own disintegrators? We could dissolve enough of the wall to maybe locate a hole that will allow us to go further."

Rhodan confessed that he had already thought about this. "It's dangerous," he said. "They might think we're attacking, and they'd retaliate. Obviously their weapons far outclass our vest pocket pea shooters."

"Well, if they're so advanced they ought to be intelligent enough to see that we're just trying to knock on the door."

Rhodan considered this.

"Well?"

Rhodan nodded. Bell lifted his small disintegrator, pointed it at the rear wall of the cave, and pressed the trigger.

Then they experienced their second surprise, which more than matched the discovery of the cave and the two giant disintegrators—the rock wall remained undisturbed!

"Damn!" Bell lowered his weapon and ran to the wall to inspect it. "It didn't even raise a blister!"

His anger and disappointment struck a funny bone in Rhodan, who had to laugh. Manoli was not any less astonished than Bell. Since he had not yet been subjected to Arkonide hypno training, he had been under the fixed impression that nothing in creation could stand up against a disintegrator.

After his first burst of anger, Bell remembered his schooling. "So *that's* what they've got!" he grumbled. "Crystal field intensification. Where do they get their power?"

Rhodan shrugged, not answering. What he had just witnessed was an advanced technique, possible against the portable weapon they were carrying, whereby the crystal structure of the matter under attack could utilize the energy to strengthen itself. But for a wall of this size—considering that it must have been protected at the moment to a depth of at least a half a yard—the energy necessary to counteract the effect of a portable disintegrator would have required a sustained output of about ten million kilowatts. That was an impressive delivery, especially considering that the wall of the cave was a very small part of the entire fortress.

Their opponent—and Rhodan began to doubt that it really was an opponent—must have at his disposal an almost inexhaustible power reserve. . . .

The robot scanner immediately observed Bell's attempt to break through the wall. Since by its own logic this could be interpreted as a hostile act, or at least an unfriendly one, it pulsed a rapid sequence of high amplitude signals to the commander to warn him of the danger.

However, as Bell had surmised, the commander possessed a sufficient faculty for decision to realize that the strangers were only seeking an entrance to the stronghold. He did not issue an order to fire but instead fell to wondering how the strangers had suspected the existence of inner chambers. At first, after he had continued to observe them for awhile, he had almost been convinced that they were primitive enough to turn around eventually and leave the cave. However, when he saw that they did not do this and that they tried to use a disintegrator to get through the rock wall, he finally realized that these beings did not belong to any of the traditional categories he knew. In view of such a circumstance, then, he had no alternative but to continue to wait and observe. . . .

The camp was notified, and orders were issued. After having returned with his own group, Tako took command. He ordered the tents to be taken down and packed, and he attended to the division of gear for transport. This time, Tako had a more difficult assignment. The rugged rock face of the mighty escarpment was not an environment that its wide beam was suited for. It had to be rerigged with an auxiliary device for heavy duty work, and its cargo carrying capacity was proportionately reduced to enable him to have a chance of making the formidable climb. Cable winches and pully gear were taken along, which Tom could power to lift himself over cliffs if the occasion called for it.

When they reached the rock chimney that served as an exhaust deflection channel by the enemy fortress, all the portable gear had to be carried up by hand. Tom waited patiently below until Tako and the three Americans had rigged the winch gear for it so that it could hoist itself up.

In spite of the obstacles, the transportation problem was overcome. Five hours after Rhodan had sent his order to the camp, all tents and equipment lay on the edge of the plateau, while Tako and all able bodied hands guided Tom in its efforts to tow itself over the low frontal wall above the exhaust tube.

Tom's entrance on the scene presented the commander of the fort with a new puzzle. Naturally, the robot scanner had spotted Tom from the first moment that it started across the lower plateau. But a detailed examination became possible only now as the ponderous machine was hoisted up onto the platform. There were discrepancies here in the levels of comparative development. Tom was out of harmony with what the scanner had observed in the strangers —with the possible exception of their clothing.

The strangers gave an impression of rashness and even primitive foolhardiness by their lack of respect for the superior technology that faced them, in the form of the giant disintegrators. Their clothing, and especially the path clearing robot machine, could not by any means represent their own handiwork. Where, therefore, were the beings who had produced the clothing and the robot, the beings who had been reported by the sea people?

The commander began to understand that these questions could only be answered by locating the spaceship—the one he had tried to pull down to the plateau with a traction beam because it was the kind of ship that his instructions had forbidden him to shoot down. But the ship had known how to escape his clutches and make a landing elsewhere— not in a location he would have preferred, but rather in some quite excellent hiding place. The information obtained from the primitive sea people had been too general for him to give more than an approximate target area to his robot spies. As a result, the ship still remained undiscovered, and the commander's curiosity remained unsatisfied.

Outside the fortress, however, some action was at last getting underway. The Earthlings stood together in front of the horse shoe shaped back wall of the plateau. They were within two yards of the gun port of the western disintegrator. The evening was approaching, and Rhodan gazed skyward with a critical eye. The cloud cover hung low above them, perhaps two or three hundred yards over their heads. He would have preferred to have located a safer shelter than the cave with its six windows.

"Well, shall we give it a try?" he asked Anne.

Anne nodded in agreement. She closed her eyes and started her mental search. For a while she did not receive any impression, but the longer she concentrated the clearer became her presentiment of what lay before her within the mountain. Naturally, this was not actual vision, but rather a probing and sensing, a scanning faculty incomprehensible to normal humans and linked with her gift of telekinesis.

Anne probed the corridor directly behind the cave wall, which led into the interior of the mountain. She presumed that where the passage had its origin behind the wall there must be a door of some kind, and she searched for the unlocking mechanism. She could discover nothing, and after a ten minute search she was too exhausted to continue.

She rested awhile and then began anew. This time she found a further passage that started from the inside of the wall about ten yards away from the first one. Here she made a new search, which ended as fruitlessly as the first. After that she found a third and a fourth passage. There was nothing in the structure of the partition wall to indicate that there were actually any doors at all, and there seemed no means of making an opening.

She pressed her mental sensitivities forward into the passages as far as she could. Her probing capacity could reach about thirty yards inward, but beyond that her impressions became muddled, the end result being that she could discover nothing. Thirty yards back the corridors were the same as they were at their beginnings. There were no intersections. There was nothing recognizable to Anne that might be a clue to their purpose or method of entry.

The entire probing operation lasted about an hour and a half. After this, Anne was so depleted that she had to be put to rest in a tent erected inside the cave. Rhodan listened closely to her, but she only murmured, "Nothing." Then she fell fast asleep.

The commander was not informed of Anne's search. The attempt of a person like this to penetrate the fortress with the bizarre faculty of telekinesis lay beyond the ability of the autoscanner to perceive. Therefore, the commander wondered at the strange inactivity of the strangers. In view of their blustering activity in the beginning, he had expected more from them than this.

CHAPTER SIX

When Anne woke up, it was near the end of another day. She had been so exhausted that she had slept almost twenty hours.

Rhodan had utilized the time, although not quite in the way he had anticipated. All the expedition's gear had been brought into the cave, and after that the gun ports had been closed with tarpaulins. There was little hope that these could withstand the storm blasts for more than a quarter of an hour, but to win that much time from such storms as Venus had to offer was quite an accomplishment.

When Anne was fully awake she reported to Rhodan what she had been able to find out about the passageways. She seemed to be discouraged and crestfallen. "You've lost a lot of precious time, haven't you?" she asked. "And because of me."

Rhodan denied this. "You are so valuable to us, Anne, that we had to let you sleep a whole day."

"I thank you for that. Are you going to send Tako inside?"

Rhodan nodded.

"Is he willing to go?"

"Yes—immediately. He's just been waiting until he could learn what information you picked up."

He went out of the tent and found Tako waiting by the cave wall. When Rhodan related Anne's observations to him, Tako indicated that he was ready.

"You have to be back here in no less than one hour," Rhodan admonished. "If you are gone longer than that we'll have to assume that something has happened to you."

Laughter broke across Tako's wide face. "And then what will you do?"

The question did not seem to embarrass Rhodan. "We'll think of something," he said. "You can count on that."

"Good! Okay, then, I'll see you in less than an hour." In the next instant, he had disappeared.

Rhodan stared gravely at the blank spot where he had been. He was certain that they could find some way to come to Tako's aid in the event that something should happen to him. However, at the moment he had no idea of what it might be.

Tako himself experienced a certain fear at this moment that caused him to shudder. He sensed a jolt as his initial teleport jump was diverted to prevent his materialization inside solid rock. A second later he came to rest. He stretched out his arm and groped at something that seemed to be like smooth, cool granite. It was completely dark here, and he knew that it would probably remain so. Also, in the complete absence of light, the eye had no means of adjusting itself to darkness. He would have to tap his way along until he could build up enough nerve to use his flashlight.

He stood there motionlessly for awhile and strained his ears, listening. But there was no more sound than there was light. It was the dead stillness of a tomb—hopefully not his own. He became aware of a strange odor that seemed to permeate the interior of the mountain. He tried to analyze what it was, but had to conclude finally that he had never sensed anything quite like it in his life.

He reached out to his right and again encountered resistance. Behind and before him was nothing; therefore, he stood in a corridor. He listened again, and as no sound reached his ears he turned on the light. He adjusted it so that it projected only a dim cone of light that was sufficient for him to orient himself but still weak enough not to be easily detected from the distance. In the pale illumination he could discover neither a termination to the passage nor anything else of an unusual nature, so he began to walk deeper into the mountain. The longer he continued without anything happening to him, the more his original anxiety lessened, and after he had walked along for about ten minutes he began to chide himself for having had the jitters.

On the other hand, Tako's intrusion was something that the autoscanner *could* react to. It transmitted the discovery to the commander in such a high amplitude chain of pulses as to rattle the equipment. The commander regarded the entrance of a single man as something that could hardly be considered dangerous. But here at last he recognized an opportunity to learn something of the strangers' intentions and their origin. And above all, here was his chance to find out about the other beings from whom these had obtained their equipment.

He feared that such revelations might not be very gratifying. Perhaps it would turn out that the strangers had taken prisoner the two beings in whom he was chiefly interested and had forced them to relinquish their equipment to them. After a quick reestimate of the available facts his assumptions seemed to him to be quite valid, and so he prepared to take stronger measures against Tako than he would have if he had completely understood the matter.

He issued an order to the security troops to capture the intruder, and they moved at once to obey. . . .

After twenty minutes of groping his way along the passage, Tako began to wonder what its purpose might be. The walls were smooth, not of natural granite, as he had thought at first, but coated with a metallic plastic that was without indentation or blemish. There were no doors, no wall mounted conduits or other devices—nothing!

Meanwhile he had dared to narrow his flashlight beam to full strength for a long throw down the passage, but as far as it could reach there was nothing to be seen. He began to reason that if he wandered long enough he must come upon another frontal wall such as the one he had left behind him and that if he were to teleport himself to its other side he would find himself out in the open on the other side of the mountain. Now what purpose could a corridor have, if it merely ran through the middle of a mountain, he asked himself.

He concentrated once more on the walls to his right and to his left, thinking that perhaps he might not have examined them sufficiently, but each wall remained smooth and seamless as before.

Inasmuch as the security police had received their instructions directly from the commander, they were well informed. For example, they knew that the intruder was apparently a natural teleporter. So it would not be enough merely to capture him; simultaneously it would be necessary to render him effectively unconscious so that he would not be able to put his strange talent to use. They also knew that he was using a source of illumination with which to light his way through the passage. Thus it would not be possible to take up a suitable position in the corridor and quietly wait for him. It was necessary to select the proper side passage and then strike at the right moment.

Last, it was also known that the intruder was armed. According to what the autoscanner had been able to determine about the type of weapon he carried, it was apparently of an advanced nature and therefore dangerous. Although the police had been created to offer their lives, if necessary, to maintain the security of the fortress, they had enough respect for their self-preservation to stay out of the path of a disintegrator.

The ten police troops posted themselves in groups of five, each of them in a side passage that intersected with the corridor through which Tako was moving. . . .

Tako was about to turn around and go back. He thought

it would serve no purpose merely to follow a miles long passageway like this. He would have preferred to have Perry Rhodan with him. Maybe Perry could have come up with an idea of how to attack these walls. He came to a stop and looked around. Before him and behind him the monotonous shaft extended—behind him about three thousand feet, and before him . . . heaven only knew how far!

He was concentrating on the cave from which he had started, intending to teleport himself there, but just then he heard a noise nearby. He turned around and stared, wide eyed, at the large opening that had appeared in the wall. Strange beings of a kind he had never seen before came into the beam of his flashlight toward him.

Perhaps he could have saved himself if he hadn't been caught between two simultaneous impulses. He didn't know whether to annihilate these beings with his disintegrator or to teleport himself out of the situation, and before he could make the decision something struck him painfully in the back, immediately paralyzing him and causing him to sink into an abyss of unconsciousness.

Instructions came promptly from the commander. "Transfer prisoner to Sector A, Level 14, Corridor 2, Room 331."

Two of the police picked up the unconscious body. The group aligned itself in formation—this time all ten in the same direction—and proceeded to carry out the order. At present they were in Sector F and on Level 21, close to the central converging point of all sectors in the circular installation. About fifty yards distant from the passage in which Tako was captured, they came to an elevator. It worked on the principle of reverse gravity, and the platform, which moved up or down in a synthetic attraction field, was large enough to accommodate all ten of the police together with their captive.

The trip downward to Level 14 lasted only a few seconds. The police turned to the right with their burden, and in the moment that they reached Room 331 in Corridor 2 and the door rolled to one side, they received the order "Prepare prisoner for interrogation!"

It became evident that the fortress had a functioning lighting system but that it was used only for special occasions such as this. Suddenly a full bank of brilliant lamps came on, suffusing the interrogation room with a pleasant, milk white light. The police laid Tako down on a piece of furniture that might have resembled a bed if it hadn't bristled with a row of strange instruments. A helmet was placed on Tako's head and a red coded wire lead from the helmet was attached to one of the instruments.

Then the commander received the announcement "Orders completed!"

Whereupon he answered, "Return to your posts!"

What Tako revealed under hypnotic questioning was a bigger surprise for the commander than he had expected. It became necessary for him to revise his idea of how the strangers had come in contact with the two beings from whom they had obtained their equipment, and this he did immediately. Of course, a thing he had to consider was that the strangers in the cave had no way of knowing about his change of opinion; yet from Tako the commander learned that they considered the fortress to be a hostile installation. So it would be a mistake merely to swing wide the doors without taking some precautions.

Therefore, he made a few preparations, and then he proceeded to establish a definite contact with the strangers.

An hour passed, and Tako had not yet returned. Rhodan became uneasy.

Meanwhile the signal code from the *Good Hope* had been received and answered. Everything seemed to be in order on board the ship. Even before they had reached the high plateau country, Rhodan and Khrest had agreed to replace the hourly radio voice contacts with a simple signal. A microsecond burst of coded data pulses was considerably more difficult to intercept and point coordinate than an extended conversation.

For similar reasons Tako was not supplied with a radio transceiver. Only Anne Sloane had been able to follow him for awhile with her mental probing faculty; but for the past fifty minutes he had remained out of her range.

Rhodan was beginning to recognize that his only alternative was to summon the *Good Hope* for help, regardless of the risk. If it could get this far without being shot down, its stronger weaponry might be able to overcome the resistance of the walls and clear a way into the interior of the mountain. The decision was a hard one, and he experienced several minutes of internal conflict to justify it. Finally he sat down at the transceiver and prepared to give a full report to Khrest and Thora and to transmit his request for help.

At that moment, Bell rushed into his tent. "The wall!" he cried out. "It's opened up!"

Rhodan came out from behind the transceiver gear and rushed out ahead of Bell. One of the others had a flashlight beam directed at one part of the wall, and within the circle of light a dark aperture gaped before them.

Rhodan did not hesitate. "Get ready to move in!" he bellowed. "Lamps, weapons, communication gear! On the double!"

He had no way of knowing how the wall had opened. Perhaps Tako had found an opening mechanism to the door; but in that case it would be hard to explain why he had not come back at the time agreed upon. Whatever the reason, he wasn't going to dally. Even if the hole was a trap, his seven man team with their complement of weapons could have some chance against the enemy.

Within a few minutes they were all ready to start. The storm was just blowing its first squalls across the plateau as they pushed into the interior of the mountain, with Rhodan in the lead. Anne Sloane walked close behind Rhodan, since he had commissioned her to keep her "feelers" out and try to sense the presence of anything that could be dangerous to them. Manoli followed with the three American astronauts, and Reginald Bell was the rear guard.

They moved along the passage about thirty yards, with Rhodan shining the beam of his flashlight from an extended arm position so as not to offer a direct target. Then, suddenly and without any announcement, a milky, shadowless light emerged from the walls and illuminated the corridor. Rhodan came to an abrupt halt; but other than the light no further surprises occurred. Perhaps, he thought, they had accidentally stepped on some sort of electrical contact.

Anne whispered suddenly, "There's a side passage behind the wall here—also behind the other wall!"

"Empty?"

She nodded.

Rhodan knew there was nothing he could do about the concealed passages. There was no more evidence of any opening mechanism here than there had been back at the cave. They'd simply have to keep on going until they found a branch corridor with a more accessible opening than these that Anne had sensed.

From here on, Anne continued to detect the presence of hidden lateral passages at regular intervals. From her continued observations Rhodan gradually constructed a mental picture of the plan of the installation. At first, Anne had sensed that the side passages led away on each side in a fairly straight line, but as they progressed she began to describe an increasing curvature. Rhodan no longer doubted that the fortress was built in a circular design. There would then be straight corridors like this, acting as a sort of spoke of a wheel running to a central hub, and circular cross-passages would join each other in a radial pattern at regular intervals, but with sharper curvature as they approached the center.

Behind the walls the radial and transverse passages probably enclosed rooms that Rhodan would have given a lot to look into. But the walls continued to reveal no sign of a door, and a short blast with the disintegrator proved that the crystal field stabilization was as effective here as it had been at the cave.

They had progressed in this manner for about a half hour, over an approximate distance of one or two miles, when Anne came to such a sudden stop that those behind her collided with her.

"Wait!" she whispered sharply.

Rhodan turned around.

"The side passage here isn't empty. There are some people standing in it!"

"People?"

Anne closed her eyes to concentrate. Her probing faculty reached out to the figures that stood on the other side of the wall and sought to determine their shape and size. They seemed strange, but no doubt remained that these unknown beings were to a large extent similar to humans. However, they did not move. They were as motionless as cadavers, causing a cold shudder to run down the girl's spine. She reported her findings to Rhodan.

"They *are* humanlike," she maintained, "but they stand there motionless as mummies!"

Rhodan decided to ignore the mysterious beings. He ordered the party to continue onward.

The commander made careful note that the group of strangers had stopped precisely at the transverse passage where he had stationed his first police unit. Was this coincidence? The autoscanner was not able to determine in what manner the strangers had become aware of the police troops. So it must have been coincidence, nothing more.

He opened an elevator door that lay in the strangers' path; then he ordered the police to go through the wall and close off the passage through which the strangers had come.

The door was about nine feet high and at least ten feet wide. Beyond it was a square room without a ceiling. Rhodan ducked his head in and immediately sensed the considerable tug at the back of his neck that the idling gravity field produced inside the shaft.

A gravity elevator.

On the walls of the lift cage there was no indication how it could be operated. Rhodan motioned to his people and instructed them to jump onto the lift platform all at once. For awhile it seemed as though the lift were not going to move. Then, however, it moved downward with such sudden swiftness that they thought someone had pulled the floor out from under them.

The trip lasted only a few seconds. Judging by the movement of the front wall of the shaft, Rhodan estimated that during that time they must have dropped over three hundred feet. No doors were spotted on the way down but when the lift suddenly stopped a door opened up before them. Here was another passage that looked no different than the one they had left. There wasn't anything at all that—

"Behind us!" Bell rasped tensely.

This time there was no need for Anne's telepathic vision. The strange beings were clearly in evidence. They stood to the left in the corridor, some sixty feet or so from the elevator, and they were motionless. Without doubt they looked like humans; yet they also seemed somehow like the spawn of hell. Their faces were discolored and pockmarked with scars, they wore no clothes, and their bodies glistened in nakedness except for the dark areas of deterioration that marked their skins.

Bell had instantly released the safety on his weapon and waited. The aliens still did not move. Rhodan separated himself from his group and went toward them. They permitted him to approach to within about thirty feet before they moved; then they lifted their arms, and Rhodan realized that they had weapons in their hands. They held the muzzles pointed directly at him.

He stared at them a moment, shrugged, and turned around.

"So we move in the other direction," he said. "Apparently that's where they want us to go."

In the other direction the corridor was empty.

"Who knows what kind of trap they're driving us into?" asked Bell in stubborn anger.

"What do you suggest?" Rhodan asked him. "Shoot it out with them at this close range? We haven't so much as a hat for cover."

"How about the elevator?"

Rhodan whirled about. The lift had disappeared, and the door had closed. The wall was again as smooth as all other walls in this place. "Damn!"

They marched to the right, and the aliens set themselves in motion, bringing up the rear of the procession. Rhodan, of course, was not happy with the situation. The passage extended ahead like a gun bore as far as he could see; nowhere was there a trace of anything that could be used for cover. If these weird beings wanted to lure his troops into a trap, that might not be as bad as having an open fight and risking the lives of his people. Passive prisoners sometimes ended up as live ones.

Apparently the fortress was swarming with aliens. If the Earthlings tried to make a stand to defend themselves at any given spot, the walls could open up and spew out a horde of reinforcements, he reasoned.

Anne began to drag her feet in weariness. The continuing tension had tired her out. Rhodan took care to support her and conserve her energies so that if he needed her help she would be able to give it.

Rhodan's somewhat reluctant pace won time for the commander to augment further his knowledge from Tako Kakuta's thought content. He learned that Tako's brain held fluent knowledge of two different languages as well as fragmentary knowledge of others. He attempted a combination of the two available complete languages in order to trace them back to some common philological root, but it didn't work. And this surprised him.

There was only one thing to do. He transmitted the new language knowledge to two of the police officers and sent them to meet the strangers.

"Halt!" ordered Rhodan as he saw the two new figures appear in the corridor before him.

The two officers approached with upraised hands. Rhodan waited for them in front of his group with his weapon ready. He noticed that these two had clear skins and that in contrast to the police unit farther down the passage behind him, they wore clothing. Also, there was no sign of pockmarks on their faces. He tried to read something from their facial expressions, but he saw nothing more than a fixed sort of smiling friendliness that was actually inscrutable, and he could draw no conclusion as to their actual intentions. The two were beardless. Their foreheads were slightly higher than the average Earthman's, but aside from this characteristic they might have been taken for Europeans, Americans, or Australians.

They came to a stop within several yards of Rhodan. One of them spoke to him in a sharp sounding, rather sing song language. Then he became silent and obviously waited for Rhodan's reply. Rhodan hadn't understood it but it seemed to sound like a strictly phonetic delivery of something like Japanese or Korean. But he didn't know either of those languages, and besides, it would be too incredible that anyone in this fortress should just happen to speak Japanese or Korean.

When he simply remained silent for a while, the other alien began to speak. This one said, "The commander requests your presence. He wishes you to know that you are welcome guests here. There is nothing to fear." Although his English was fluent and without an accent, his voice sounded a bit flat and the words were delivered in a strange sort of monotone.

Rhodan remained mystified for only a fraction of a second. While others in his party commented in surprise, he quickly perceived what had happened—either they had captured Tako or he was willingly cooperating with them, and they had drawn from his mind the two languages that he spoke.

Rhodan weighed these factors in some desperation. There still wasn't any good reason to believe that the fortress commander was not playing games. In support of some sort of deception, the invitation would of course be politely worded. If he were setting a trap for them, naturally it would save him a lot of trouble if they all simply accepted his nice sounding proposition and went along with the officers.

In spite of this, Rhodan answered, "We are very much obliged to your commander. Will you kindly lead us to him."

The English speaking officer made an about-face and started walking with his companion back in the direction he had come from. Rhodan and his group followed.

Rhodan turned his head slightly to his people and spoke rapidly in low tones. "Everybody on their toes now. I don't know if they're going to try to get cute with us or play it straight."

He heard a mutter of grim assent from the men, and Bell added, "We should have asked them about Tako."

"Not the time for it now," Rhodan retorted swiftly.

The diffused light of the passageway made it difficult to judge distances. Up until now the passage had seemed to be capable of running along straight without end, but only a few minutes after the meeting with the alien officers, the outlines of new objects began to take shape before them. A few moments later the passage opened into a chamber of unusual dimensions.

At first glance the place seemed to form a rectangle that stretched at least five hundred yards to the right and left, with an approximate width of two hundred yards, but they finally determined that the whole area was actually a colossal access way surrounding a circular building that stood in its center, as though this were a civic square before some sort of government structure.

The two aliens walked across the "square," and the Earthmen followed them. Rhodan noted with some astonishment that the gigantic chamber must have measured about a hundred and sixty feet in height and that in its surrounding walls there were galleries at even intervals in which the corridors of the fortress terminated at their respective levels. They were obviously approaching the stronghold's inner sanctum, and Rhodan wondered what they would find in the interior of the circular building.

The building seemed not only to be as lofty as the chamber but to extend even through its ceiling. Its wall was as smooth and devoid of seams as all other walls in the fortress, but when they reached it the wall parted before them and gave them a full view of a tremendous room that was illuminated considerably more brightly than other areas they had seen thus far.

In spite of its size, the room seemed to occupy only a fractional part of the entire building. When Rhodan stepped through the wide opening, he recognized at first glance what the rest of the building consisted of and what its purpose was.

The rear wall of the room—about a hundred feet wide and fifty feet high—was a single gigantic control panel quite similar to the smaller panel in the control room of the *Good Hope*. A kind of control console projected out about eight feet from it, and to the right and left of this were a number of suspended platforms, obviously designed for carrying operators easily upward to any desired location on the titanic panel.

Rhodan was convinced on the spot that this control room must be a part of the greatest positronic robot brain that had ever been constructed anywhere in the galaxy.

The two aliens stopped when they reached the middle of the room. They waited until Rhodan and the others arrived beside them; then one of them pointed at the giant control panel and spoke with great formality.

"This is the commander. He is happy to see you."

What followed were days of uninterrupted revelation of the astounding technical wonders hidden within the mountain. Although Bell and Rhodan were somewhat prepared for such surprises by virtue of their Arkonide training, they were nevertheless jolted over the fact that all this was to be found on Venus, of all places. The crowning revelation of all, as Rhodan had immediately suspected in spite of his incredulity, was given to them by the commander himself, who was as hungry for knowledge as they were. The stronghold had been built long ago by the race to which Khrest and Thora belonged—in short, by the Arkonides. After Rhodan had reported his discovery to Khrest and Thora, they blasted off immediately in the *Good Hope* and landed unharmed on the plateau before the cave.

For Rhodan it was practically a major event to see Khrest become genuinely bewildered, for the first time since he had known him. To Khrest it was completely incredible that a chapter of the Arkonide colonial history should have escaped the central Arkon register, however insignificant or remotely separated by time. Rhodan's rather tongue in cheek reminder that even the most sophisticated computer ever created was capable of pulling a booboo once in a while went over like a lead balloon with Khrest, because it smacked too much of the Earthly human brand of thinking, with which he could never associate his vaunted race.

For Khrest, the so called commander was the greatest positronic robot brain he had ever seen outside of the central brain on Arkon. It placed at his disposal its entire historical file, into which he plunged with the utmost zeal. The data were retrieved in the form of oral reports in a language that the *Good Hope*'s robot translator had earlier defined as archaic Rim Galacto and also in the form of video strips or pulse patterns whose contents were transmitted by methods similar to those used in hypno training.

Inadvertently, Khrest performed a time saving service for Rhodan and Bell, inasmuch as he restricted himself to take stock of the vast historical data, which freed Rhodan and Bell to concentrate on exploring the physical aspects of their surroundings. Armed with further information that Khrest obtained, they investigated the mighty fortress level by level, sector by sector, and passage by passage, compiling a complete inventory of everything. It required only a rough survey of several hours, actually, to arrive at the conclusion that enough usable equipment and material were available here to bridge the Third Power over all remaining difficulties of its young existence.

After Tako Kakuta had recovered from the rigors of his

hypnotic questioning he was set free and, like the rest of the scouting party, assigned a room on Level 10. The others passed their time as they pleased in the long corridors and great rooms of the fortress. After receiving the necessary instructions, they found that the glass smooth walls and their hidden doors presented no further obstacle to them. Although their activity was reduced to a rather blundering and childlike groping about in this technological wonderworld they were at least relieved to find that the commander had withdrawn his pockmarked naked police troops, so that they wouldn't be startled by running into them anywhere.

The police force consisted of nothing else than robots that had withstood the ravages of time since the fortress had been built. The stronghold did not harbor a single living being. It consisted of the commander—a giant positronic computer brain—and his army of automatons, nothing more. The self-perpetuating robotic maintenance section had provided that everything withstood the millennia without significant damage. Of course, the commander had not considered the synthetic skin coverings of his robots to be of such importance as to have them continuously refurbished, and this was why their organic plastic flesh appeared discolored and had developed small holes, or pockmarks, as the Earthmen called them. The robot officers were an exception, owing to their considerably more complex functions.

Finally one day Khrest emerged from the learning and research chambers. He was tired; yet his eyes gleamed triumphantly, and he announced that he was ready to brief all members of the scouting party on what he had gleaned from the stronghold's computer memory banks. This method of communicating the information was necessary since none of the terrestrials, outside of Bell and Rhodan, was at present capable of receiving the more direct input of Arkonide hypno impulses from the positronic machine.

They were brought together in the main room, where the giant brain's control panel occupied one wall. Everyone was present except Thora. Since the first day when the *Good Hope* had landed outside on the plateau, Thora had seldom been seen. Rhodan was fairly certain what she was seeking, and since he had meanwhile become more familiar with the technical data of the fortress than she, he felt sorry for her and her foolish hope.

Khrest delivered his report in English; he had learned it perfectly now, and no one could catch him in the slightest language error. "This base," he began, "is by your time reckoning about ten thousand years old. According to the galactic history of the Arkonide Empire, it stems from the period of the First Colonization.

"Originally the colonial fleet that landed here had another goal in mind. They had interrupted their flight to examine the third planet, since it appeared to be a more desirable harbor than the world their star charts had originally indicated as being suitable for a new colony. But when they visited the third planet—your own Earth—and found it to be inhabited, they decided to land first on Venus and prepare a supply base from which to organize the settlement of Earth. From this decision evolved the present fortress in which we now find ourselves.

"The Arkonides—the record speaks of some two hundred thousand of them—settled a continent on Earth that, according to my knowledge, no longer exists today. Ten thousand years ago, that continent consisted of the fragment of a great isthmus that once connected the land masses of Africa, Europe, and the Western Hemisphere.

"Unfortunately, the colonial empire thus established was of short duration. The causes of the natural catastrophe that destroyed it and brought general calamity to the entire planet are details that you can familiarize yourselves with later; the point is that only about five percent of the Arkonides escaped the catastrophe and were able to return here to Venus.

"At that time the Venus base possessed at least half a fleet of space worthy vessels—space worthy in the sense that the ships were capable of jumping almost any interstellar distance with an almost negligible expenditure of time. The colonists . . . Ah, but wait a moment! At this point perhaps I should insert an explanation of something else.

"The colonization flights were never very democratic operations—they couldn't be. During the early years of the founding and rise of empire, our young colonies had to have firm guidance. It became a standing principle with us that such guidance would always be achieved best through a ruling structure of the aristocracy. So it was that an aristocratic Royal Council decided that the colonial survivors should set out in the remaining ships to reach their original goal, since for centuries to come Earth would be unsuitable for another attempt at colonization, due to the cataclysm that had changed it. The decision was carried out, as naturally there could be no debate against the decrees of the Royal Colonial Council, and the major number of the colonists departed from Venus in the ships of the remaining fleet. A small number remained behind because there was no room for them on the ships. Some two thousand of them had to stay here. They led a somewhat lonely but certainly not uncomfortable life. Apparently the Council had done this on a selective basis, leaving behind those who were the most sluggish intellectually. This judgment was substantiated by the fact that the castaways made no attempt to utilize the ample materials and equipment that lay at their disposal, for the purpose of building more spaceships. They simply remained where they were. About eight thousand years ago, the last of them died out.

"The colonization of this sector of the galaxy seems to have been ill fated from its inception. The survivor fleet that set out from Venus was never heard from again. We are certain that they never reached their goal, but of course, no one knows what happened to them. Arkon has never picked up any trace of them, and also this Venusian positronic brain—the so-called commander—has nothing to offer in this regard.

"Being self sufficient, this present base continued operating automatically. Its robotic maintenance facilities were capable of keeping all equipment in a perfectly functioning condition. It has survived the millennia, and the only way it ever betrayed its presence here was the hot air exhaust from its reactors, on a ten hour cycle, through a cleverly camouflaged deflection channel outside the mountain.

"The positronic brain continued to operate in accordance with the final instructions that had been given to it by the last Arkonide commander. By means of the continuously active robot scanner and coordinate locator equipment, it kept in contact with the developing Venusian intelligences —that is, with the sea people, or seal creatures.

"Also, the brain was instructed either to force all spaceships to land or to destroy them, but Arkonide ships were an exception. This was based on the assumption that any Arkonide ships flying to this planet and having something to do with the colonization of this sector would be able to respond with the local zone's code signal to the brain's IFF transmissions—a query that we failed to understand when we approached. But even though we did not reply properly, the commander—the positronic brain—was able to recognize that our ship was the kind that it was not permitted to shoot down. It attempted to draw us to the plateau with the traction beam, but"—he made a slight bow in Rhodan's direction—"*our* commander succeeded, by virtue of his fast reaction, in circumventing the gravitic forces and landing us in a place where the brain was not able to find us. So it got in touch with the seal creatures and sought to determine our location by means of their information. This attempt also failed, because the sea people were not intelligent enough to furnish the kind of coordinate data that the brain could evaluate.

"So it was that the brain waited patiently and a few days later was able to determine that the 'strangers,' as it had designated the raiding team, were coming to it of their own volition. The brain started registering some very astonishing details; these intruders were actually aliens to its way of thinking, but their equipment was largely of Arkonide origin. The brain concluded that you people had succeeded in overpowering an Arkonide ship and in capturing and robbing its crew. This analysis, however, still lacked certain elements of probability, so it continued to watch and study your approach. A few hours later, Tako teleported himself right into its hands, and the brain saw its opportunity. Tako was captured and subjected to questioning under hypnosis. The rest you know."

Khrest leaned back in his seat and waited until its structure adjusted itself to his form. His listeners were silent. For the members of a race whose written history went back only about five thousand years, it made an impression on them to hear a member of a much older race speak of a multithousand year epoch out of the history of a branch of his people as though it were merely a trifling detail.

Rhodan was less impressed with the report, per se, but he was left pensive and almost in awe of the fact that here

—out of the preserved ancient records of an extraterrestrial race of intelligences—the first actual proof of the existence of the fabled empire of Atlantis had emerged. Nothing else could be concluded from the report of a colonial empire settling on a fragmentary land bridge between Africa, Europe, and the Western Hemisphere. A smile touched Rhodan's lips as he realized that the Arkonides, who just one year ago had been forced by circumstance to land on the moon, were not only a priceless boon to present Earth technology but also the same in an equal degree for the fields of history, because with their own actual records they were able now to clarify one of the dimmest areas of human history so that no questions remained.

He noted that Khrest had again risen to his feet, and it broke his train of thoughts.

"The brain," Khrest began once more, "has thus been waiting here for eight thousand years. That in itself is relatively unimportant; but our brain here"—he jerked his thumb over his shoulder—"had an objective to accomplish. It has waited for a new commander—a human director whose mental makeup would be such that it could lock its mental impulses into complete rapport with him and thus obey only his commands. As it now appears, the brain has actually found this new commander. . . ."

He paused to observe the effect of his words on the others. His listeners looked at each other in bewilderment. Khrest's slow, laconic smile seemed to indicate that he had a big surprise in store—but who could it be? It was no more than reasonable to believe that an Arkonide positronic brain would choose as its new master a person who most resembled its original creators in the mental and psychological sense—in other words, Khrest, or perhaps Thora.

Khrest smirked at them. "I know what you're thinking, but you deceive yourselves—or maybe not. Through Tako, and much more through my own information, mental data on every member of this expedition are known to the brain. The future commander of this base cannot be mentally distinguished from an Arkonide, although he happens to be an Earthman: *Perry Rhodan!*"

It took Rhodan a few seconds to recover from this surprise. Not that he underestimated his own qualifications, but he was taken back by the consequences inferred by the brain's decision, and he was wondering if Khrest might have fibbed a little to the positronic monster.

He then realized, however, that no one could pull the wool over the eyes of a cosmic scale computer like this, so he finally squared up to an acceptance of the honor. For a while he feared that Khrest might take a dim view of the brain's expressed preference, but apparently Khrest, as a true scientist, was above being envious when it came to more or less political issues.

So it was that Rhodan became the commander, or supreme sovereign, of a great stronghold that concentrated in its small area more power and energy than all the factories and research centers of the Earth combined. With the tremendous facilities of this Venusian base, entire solar systems could be annihilated, and any alien enemy could be repelled—that is, provided he didn't invade with a massive fleet.

There was one thing, however, that the base did *not* possess. . . .

Thora had not wanted to accept the reality of it. After her personal contact with the positronic brain during the first hours of their arrival, she had obtained a complete rundown on the detailed location of every nook and cranny of the fortress, and then she had set out on her search.

A few hours after Rhodan's assumption of the post of commander, and after his brainwave patterns had been programmed into the positronic entity so that it could respond only to his commands, he ran into Thora.

He and Bell had been investigating some storage rooms in the highest level of the installation. They had switched on only a portion of the light banks, and Thora emerged out of the darkness like an ethereal materialization. She was unusually pale, and as both men perceived the pride that restricted her emotions, she presented a picture of tragedy. As she came up to him, Rhodan gently placed his hand on her shoulder. She did not withdraw from his touch.

"You're on the wrong trail," he said gravely, knowing full well what troubled her.

Thora appeared to sense that he had perceived her objective. "I know," she answered faintly.

"Why don't you try to look at the facts?" he asked her.

"You know that when the colonists decided to continue on in search of their original goal, after the Atlantis cataclysm, they took all the ships with them that were available. This stronghold is a marvelous grab bag to serve *my* purposes; but there's nothing here that could help *you*, if you're thinking of traversing the unthinkable distances between here and your home planet of Arkon."

He paused and waited for her great eyes to turn to his. Then he smiled and continued, "For the time being, you have to consider yourself as Earthbound, more or less. I will do everything possible to make your sojourn as pleasant as I can, and I'll also do everything in my power to speed you on your way home. But even the swiftest way still represents a matter of a few years yet. Meanwhile, you'll just have to live with us half savages!"

"Oh! Will you please be silent!" she exclaimed in an unexpected burst of vehemence. "Do you propose to be the only being in the universe who has never made a mistake?"

The Radiant Dome

CHALLENGE FROM THE STARS . . .

Perry Rhodan had returned from the moon in Spaceship Stardust accompanied by two of the Arkonides. But the earth was on the verge of an atomic conflict. So Perry Rhodan, Peacelord of the Universe, threw an impregnable forcefield around the Stardust and declared his ship independent of the warring nations.

As he had hoped, the holocaust was temporarily averted by the more deadly threat of his allies from the stars; but could Perry Rhodan keep the peace long enough to persuade the Arkonides that mankind was fit to enter their galactic community?

THE RADIANT DOME is the second novel in the world's bestselling S.F. series. Don't miss Perry Rhodan's first cosmic adventure, ENTERPRISE STARDUST.

The Face in the Abyss

A remote valley hidden amid the towering peaks of the Andes and never before visited by civilised man is the scene of A. A. Merritt's classic novel of supernatural fantasy. The valley is inhabited by creatures long forgotten and races pledged to the resurrection of the glorious past.

Into this valley stumbles a young mining engineer, Nicholas Graydon. He defies the commands of the Snake-Mother's invisible but deadly servants and returns to the forbidden valley for the sake of Suarra, whom he loves. But Suarra can not be his until Graydon has persuaded the Snake-Mother to free the land of Yu-Atlanchi from Nimir, the Shadow of Evil. And the way to the Snake-Mother is beset with perils. Such as Lantlu, rider of dinosoaurs; the Lizard men. And, of course, the Dark Lord himself.

Dwellers in the Mirage

Beneath the shimmering surface of a lake cradled in the desolate Alaskan mountains, the people of the Shadowed-Land waited for Dwayanu, the warrior hero who will bring back to the world the worship of Khalk'ru, the cruel, destructive octopus god whose appetites must be appeased by human sacrifice.

When Lief Langdon accidentally discovers the people beneath the valley floor, they welcome him as the reincarnation of Dwayanu. Slowly Langdon's personality is possessed by the pride and blood-lust of his warrior ancestor until he is driven by forces beyond his understanding or control to serve the evil power of Khalk'ru.

A classic of science fiction, DWELLERS IN THE MIRAGE weaves a powerful web of fantasy against a background of lost civilisations.

Enterprise Stardust

PERILOUS DAWN . . .

Major Perry Rhodan, commander of the spaceship
STARDUST, found more than anyone had expected
might exist on the moon — for he became the first
man to make contact with another sentient race!

The Arkonides had come from a distant star, and
they possessed a knowledge of science and
philosophy that dwarfed mankind's knowledge.

But these enormously powerful alien beings
refused to cooperate with the people of Earth . . .
unless Perry Rhodan could pass the most difficult
test any human being had ever faced . . .

ENTERPRISE STARDUST is the first novel
in the Perry Rhodan series which sold
more than 70 million copies in
Europe and America.